Dream Big Publishing
Byron Center, MI

This book is a work of fiction. Any references to historical events, real people, or real locales are used factiously. Other names, characters, places, and incidents are the product of the author's imagination, and any resemblance to actual events or locales or persons, living or dead, is entirely coincidental.

Dream Big Publishing
A publication of Dream Big Publishing
Byron Center MI
Copyright 2014 by Lindsey Owens
All rights reserved, including the right of reproduction in whole or in part in any form.
Dream Big Publishing is a registered trademark of Dream Big Publishing.
Text of this book is set in Garamond text size 13.
Manufactured in the United States of America
All rights reserved.

Summary: Miley is still young, but she is somewhat successful. She is about to give up on her workplace and search for something better. Since she was cheated on, Miley does not trust any man. Her boss is a sexist pig and she's had enough, until he offers the chance of a lifetime, to go photograph an exotic island that has never been explored before.

The island is mysterious, exotic and gorgeous. Part of the Galapagos Islands, the land is amazing. But this place may be far more than Miley could have expected. It seems to be filled with unexpected creatures and men who vie for her affection when she wants nothing more than to do her job and get home. Will they begin to wear her down? Will they let her go home back to the city and a life she was not that fond of anyway?

Find out what happens when the alpha finds out who actually sent her to photograph and will a war between two clans soon follow?

[1. Dragons – Fantasy Fiction 2. Romance]
ISBN: 978-1497423947
Lindsey Owens
Copyright 2014 by Lindsey Owens
All rights reserved.

DEDICATION

To all those who have supported me. My family, my friends, and my wattpad readers. Thank you everyone.

Chapter 1

"Miley!" Charles called. Miley stopped mid step, her long brunette hair swishing over her shoulders. She was through with Siegel Images. After six months of disappointment, she was bored here. Everything was the same, bare land two miles from the city or a vacant lot five inches from their building; she hasn't had the opportunity to find something interesting. This was far from what she had been offered originally and even farther from what she had hoped for out of her experience.

"What is it, Charles?" Miley groaned. She tipped her head back slightly letting out a sigh as she pinched the bridge of her nose. She turned around and pushed her hands down the length of her pristine multi-colored dress and looked confidently up into his cold eyes.

Charles was far from her type of man. He was stiff and boring, not to mention a complete dork. His dark hair was combed to the side and thick glasses adorned his thin pointed nose. Miley had yet to figure out why he was such a sexist pig and prick; she was sure he really could not get any woman to look his way. Charles tugged nervously at his grey suit and cleared his throat.

"I can't do this without you," his voice betrayed stiffened cold form, he was defeated. Could he really be turning a new leaf? Would he try to become a nicer boss? Would he let her do the job she was hired to do? The thought flashed in her mind for a moment, and her features lit up slightly. "Uh…" he said. "You know I can't let a woman do any more than you already do."

"That's exactly why I am leaving!" Miley shouted with fervor. "You're so sexist."

"I'm not sexist, Miley; it's just a fact that men are better at dealing with our type of clients," he tried to reason.

"I'm done." Miley shook her head while backing down the hall as she sneered at him. She wasn't going to let Charles push her back with condescension into the position she was fighting to get out of.

"Wait!" he begged, rubbing his hand through his hair and looking down at his feet. Miley could tell her leaving was raking Charles's thoughts. "What if I give you a place to check out…" he asked looking up at her. "Would you stay…? A raise maybe?"

This was Miley's chance. She knew Charles knew better than to let her go. Finding someone with her experience and background was unlikely. He would be looking for months, maybe even longer to find someone who was as unique as she was, and he knew it. Loser. He should not have been such a prick and hit on her at every chance. Ha!

"Why?" Miley said. She just had to do it… she had to know what his reason was.

Charles shrugged. "I just don't think a man can pull it off."

Miley rolled her eyes. "I am not going to use sex appeal." Miley grunted.

"That's not it…" Charles said almost too quickly.

She had caught it though and raised an eyebrow at him. "Uh… I … Okay… Fine," Charles puffed. "They have turned down nearly twenty men for the contract. I just thought…"

"What kind of place?" she asked coolly. Miley was calm and relaxed; she could easily walk off this job and get another within a short period of time. Heck, she had even thought of starting her own freelance photography and digital images company. She had plans for her life and they were not just to sit and waste away.

Miley had been considering leaving since she broke it off with Toby. It seemed like paperwork was all she did lately for Charles and his cronies.

"This is a very special client. One I was going to give to Peter but…" Charles wavered slightly. "Look, Peter turned it down. He said there is no way he would be interested in traveling to such a remote place to take picture of rocks and trees. I'm desperate here." Charles sighed, his shoulders slumped, and he leaned back against the wall for support.

"Ah… the truth finally comes out." Miley laughed.

"I'll double your pay, cut the hours if you wish… and I'll try my best to let you choose first dibs on assignments if you would like as well. I just need you to stay," Charles begged.

"Let me see the file." Miley groaned for effect, but she had to give him some credit. He was offering to double her pay, which was awesome. Not like, she needed it. She worked for entertainment, really. Though she wasn't quite sure she could believe the man on the fairness and first dibs part, but… double the pay… she might have to give it a shot.

Miley held out her hand, waiting for Charles to pass over the file he had held tightly in his grip. Charles grinned, stretching out his hand and quickly moving forward toward her. "It's," he began.

"Just. Let. Me. Look," Miley drawled snatching the file from his grasp.

"I will be in my office," she told him. She hadn't cleared it out yet. She had just told him she was quitting this morning.

Therefore, Miley turned and sauntered her butt down the hallway toward the horribly small office. "I'll have to demand a new office too…" Miley smirked as she muttered to herself. She had Charles right where she wanted him; groveling and desperate.

She flicked on the light and then closed the door; walking around to the back of her desk, she curled herself into her office chair. Sitting up slightly to push herself toward the desk, she reached out and opened the file.

Chapter 2

The pictures of the island were gorgeous, tropical, and unique. The problem was that there weren't many of them, just two. Miley was actually quite surprised when she looked at it. Most of the normal clients would have been bragging about such beauty.

There wasn't much in the file, simply contact information for the magazine company and what type of photos they were searching for, also directions on how to get to the island. It seemed that there was hidden beauty on this remote island, and the magazine wanted to uncover it.

The magazine company stated that they knew Miley would be the right person for the job. They had looked through her portfolio multiple times. Miley had begun to make a name for herself without the help of Siegel Images. She had become known to get the inside scoop and to discover things that other photographers had missed.

Miley felt that she had to go and explore the place. The rarity of anyone ever exploring the island made it just so tempting. This was a newly discovered unexplored island, what opportunities were waiting for her? Thinking about this made her wonder what they were really looking for.

Notes in the file had mentioned that the magazine company requested images of said island, of stone structures, rare animals, and unique features. The magazine was known for bringing new discoveries to people all over the world through their magazine.

Opening her computer and email... Miley began to type frantically.

Dear Geography Decoded Magazine,

I am the elusive photographer, Miley Tanner from Siegel Images. I would love the opportunity to travel and explore the island in question. To add to the contract, I would like to propose full photo and digital rights, royalties at seventy percent. If these terms are agreeable, I could leave out later this week.

Sincerely,

Miley Tanner

The email was sent. Miley folded the laptop back closed and waited.

She sighed. Why could not she get something more descriptive? She pushed her chair back as she closed the file, snatching it up, and stored it in the top drawer of her filing cabinet before leaving. Charles could wait until after lunch for her reply. She wanted to wait and see if the magazine company would reply. She did not want to call.

Outside, the streets were busy. New York had always been busy, let alone at lunchtime. Miley walked up to her favorite vender and smiled. "Hey, Walt, what's on the menu today?"

Walt smiled brightly "Well, I have bbq, soup, and I know you probably don't want those so... just for my favorite client grilled chicken salad."

"Awe... thanks. I knew I can always count on you for the best lunches," Miley gushed. She had been getting her lunches from Walt a few days a week for years now. He was such a wonderful old man. He seemed a lot like a grandfather to her.

"So, how did quitting the job go?" he asked with a slight chuckle. Miley had been complaining for a while now and seriously threatening to leave for the last week.

"I think Charles just offered me an opportunity I could not refuse," she shrugged.

"Really now?" Walt raised an eyebrow and smirked.

"NO, you sick old man… not like that," she blushed.

"Well, I just figured you're such a beautiful woman and he's been trying to get your attention ever since you started…" Walt suggested.

"I am not crazy enough to smooze with Charles," Miley shuddered.

"It might be a great offer for a young woman like you…" Walt chuckled.

"Anyways," Miley laughed. "He offered double pay, an all-inclusive trip to an exotic island, which has never been explored, and I am going to get that corner office away from him," she smiled proudly.

"Good girl," Walt smiled. "I knew you'd do it. Now get back there and tell Charles whose boss," Walt encouraged.

Miley grasped the salad, then handed Walt his money before she turned around and to walk back toward the office.

She stopped for a moment. "Walt… if I am not around for a while, don't get worried. I might be going on that trip soon," She told him before rushing back and offering a tight hug. "Bye, gramps," she snickered before trotting away, her stilettos clicking as she left.

As Miley went into her office to eat her delicious salad, she noticed a very angry looking Peter stomping down the hall. 'I wonder what got into him,' she thought.

After eating, Miley ditched her container in the trash. She pulled the computer toward her and lifted up the computer's top. Surprisingly, there was a message from the magazine

Dear M. Tanner,

The terms are perfectly agreeable and we have booked you a flight to the Galapagos for Saturday morning. A guide will greet you as you land.

Eagerly awaiting your photos

Miley smiled then went to seek out Charles. People started to wonder what was up as she confidently strode down the hall, but Miley did not care. She could very easily explain everything in a meeting later, when she got back, and, other than that, it wasn't their business anyway.

Miley knocked once before she pushed open the door. "Ms. Tanner you can't..." the secretary screeched.

Miley did not listen. She continued inside ignoring receptionist.

"Miley... uh..." Charles stuttered out as a blond lifted her head up from between his legs on the far side of the desk.

"Miley? I'm Jill," The blond scolded before she realized Miley was standing there.

"I am glad you finally moved on Charles." Miley snickered "Anyway, I'll take the client. In fact, I will be flying out first thing Saturday morning. Oh, and I get the corner office, right."

"That's Peter's office," Jill giggled dumbly.

"Not anymore," Miley rolled her eyes at the idiot.

"The one with all the windows," she smirked her tone just begged him to disagree, it would be amusing.

Charles' head slightly nodded "Anything," he straggled out. "This client's very important, I can't lose them."

"I figured. Well, I guess I'll make plans to leave," Miley told him. "I expect that raise and that bonus to reach my checking account before Saturday, or I guess we can forget the client," Miley shrugged as she went out the door. Just for good measure, she left the door wide open and turned her head back to say, "Oh, by the way, Jill, you could do so much better than sucking his pencil."

The secretary gasped and Miley was sure she nearly shit her pants as she continued down the hall. Many of the wondering faces turned toward her in shock and surprise as they tried to gather around Charles' door and catch a sight of Jill between his legs.

Ever since Toby's cheating, Miley could not help but feel hatred for most men. Charles was not an exception.

Chapter 3

It was Saturday morning, and sure enough, a big fat bonus, along with a pay raised check, hit Miley's bank account. She could not help but smile at how generous Charles turned out to be; a five grand bonus along with her already hefty pay raised check was something to not complain about.

Miley's flight had been scheduled for Saturday. She was still extremely busy but took the day off Friday so she could shop and pack. She hadn't been on a trip since her honeymoon with Toby, so most of her things needed to be upgraded.

Miley had shopped, finding a black and pink suitcase, two new swimsuits, and a few spring wrap dresses. She already owned plenty of outfits, but she figured it would be good to get something new that would work well with the sunshine of a tropic island.

Miley knew she wouldn't need much in the lines of cold weather clothing so all she brought was one sweatshirt. One always need to be prepared, right? Miley had decided on sandals and a pair of tennis shoes for her shoes, and she packed her bag with all the hiking gear she could think of.

The magazine company had told her the guide would provide her with cooking supplies, a tent, food, and blankets; all of which would be hard for Miley to take on the plane. Other than that, Miley had packed her clothing, notepads and pencils, her camera and lots of extra charged batteries. She also packed her ipod and solar charging dock for everything.

Miley's bag was packed and she was ready to go by eight pm on Friday. She had her big suitcase packed with all of her clothing and the other items she thought that she would need.

The taxi arrived early and Miley walked out to greet the man with a smile. "Hello. How is traffic today?"

"It's just like any other day in New York. Let's just get movin' so that we don't get stuck in it," he scoffed.

"Of course," she said then slid into the back seat of the yellow cab while the driver placed her bags in the back.

The drive, like any other, came with its complications. People encroached on the roads; cars were all over, but the cab arrived with plenty of time. "Thanks," Miley cooed as she grabbed hold of her two bags and tugged them away.

The airport was as if she had remembered it, huge. Miley pushed her way through the crowd until she came to the pre-bought-ticket booth. "I have a reserved ticket. Miley Tanner. One to the Galapagos Islands," she told the woman behind the counter.

"Yes. I see you here. One luggage, one carry-on," she said typing rapidly. "First class. Prepaid."

"Yes, that's it," Miley smiled.

"Can I see some identification and passport?" she asked.

"Sure," Miley murmured scrounging in her purse where she had stored them.

"Thank you," The ticket woman said sounding as if she had plugged her nose to reply. "Okay. Thank you, Miss Tanner. The plane is AirGul, down that way to gate sixty-five. Its flight number 140 and it boards at 9:05."

"Thanks," Miley muttered as she pushed her ID and passport back into her purse along with the lonely ticket. She looked down at her watch and then up to the clock for confirmation. She had forty minutes to get there. Deciding she would get a latte before her flight, she took off toward the food court.

Miley made her way down the corridor while she sipped gingerly at her drink. When she finally got to the gate, she sat down on the benches and waited.

Chapter 4

"I received an email from Geography Decoded Magazine," the man said to his alpha.

"Well, that's great," He smiled to his second in command. "What did they say?"

"They said thank you for the tip and there is a person on their way to discover what secrets lay there," the man smiled devilishly. "They're sending someone to investigate the island, take pictures, and hopefully he will catch sight of one of them."

"Perfect," the other man beamed at his second in command. They had long since been looking for a way to destroy the other clan, and this was the perfect attack. Nobody would suspect it was them.

"Your plan is going to work perfectly," the man chuckled. "Now. Let us see how this plays out. Maybe we can get the alpha female after all."

"What do you want me to do about the person… the magazine company wanted me to guide him," the beta asked nervously.

"That's more than obvious Victor," the alpha snorted.

"Pick him up at the airport and drop him off at the island. When the bags are tossed off the boat hightail it out of there."

"Yes alpha," the man nodded.

 "Great," the edges of the alpha's lips rose slightly. He was hoping that they would send someone and not look at the tip as a hoax. "And when does this man arrive?"

"Well, I received a confirmation from the magazine, he's arriving tomorrow. I guess his flight was leaving New York in the United State on Saturday as I understood it."

"Good, you're free to go now," The alpha chuckled darkly. He was evil. If he had to expose his own kind to rid himself of the clan stronger than his then… so be it.

"And Victor…" the alpha's called stopping Victor from leaving.

"Yes, alpha," Victor said quickly turning toward his alpha.

"I want to have a meeting with all the clan tonight, six pm we'll have a potluck," the alpha told him.

Chapter 5

As the Alpha prepared for the pending clan meeting, he could not help, but feel the tension building around him. Everyone seemed to have shown up, and it was great. Clan members were anxious to hear his news. Yet, he could feel that many were beyond nervous.

"Hello, everyone!" the alpha boomed over the crowd.

"Alpha," Victor bowed his head as he approached, taking his place beside the podium. "Everyone has come to hear the announcements."

The alpha nodded down to his second in command. "Thank you everyone for coming. I know you all have questions, but I will direct questions to Victor later. I have devised a plan. We have contacted a magazine to explore the Isle of Myst," gasps erupted around the room and the alpha sighed.

The group did not really know what to think. They were worried about being exposed. Their homes were secluded, hidden in the jungles of South America.

"They will be sending a photographer."

More gasps. Really people, the alpha groaned, but then continued, "If our plan works well... the McBride Clan will be exposed."

Everyone began to murmur worriedly. The alpha could hear their complaints and worries. His speech had lasted nearly a half an hour, and his stomach was rumbling. The alpha made his way to the head of the line and filled his plate up with the best of the treats on the table.

Once dinner was done, the alpha made his way to the ocean's shore. "Take flight with me?" he called out hearing multiple roars behind him. Many of the clan had already shifted and were awaiting him. The alpha smiled. "Soon we will not need to worry, we can claim the Isle for our own!" he called.

He could feel the creature within him weaving around his body anxiously. It crept up from the markings, similar to a tattoo sprawling across his arm, chest, and back, until it finally burst from his skin. The spirit form took flight, swirling around him as alpha lifted his head to the sky and sucked in a deep breath. "Take me," he commanded. Not even seconds later, it burst through him, shifting his body to become the creature, his true form.

Massive wings thumped through the air. They lifted up the massive beasts attached to them. It was a unique and beautiful sight, if only there was anyone here to watch. The only ones watching the beasts take flight were their human counter-parts, which had seen the sight many times.

One of the beasts roared, alerting the others that they were to turn around and hover over the island. Before they landed, the biggest and strongest of the beasts chuffed, tilting his head. His second in command turned his head in the direction of which his alpha tilted his head. A sacrificial ceremony was about to take place.

One of them was expected to come and kill the woman on the platform. She was to die with a purpose. She would be providing the safety of the surrounding villages, and the people living there.

It was the choice of the alpha that tonight he would do it. It was a risky task, which only experienced warriors took on. The massive grey green beast broke away from his group letting his beta direct the clan back home.

The villagers were all locked safely within their homes. They were terrified. Petrified even; afraid the beast would eat them as well. They did not dare look out the windows because rumors about the beast instilled such fear… they wouldn't dream of catching sight of its ugly, terrifying form.

The night was getting late, and the dragon was assured the sacrifice would be drooping against the hefty ropes they would have tied her with. If he did not get there quickly, blood would be shed from cuts the ropes would produce. That was just something which really had no purpose; there was no reason to spill the blood.

As the whoop of his massive wings sounded through the air, the sacrifice looked up, fear evident in her eyes.

She was just as beautiful as any of the others had been. This one was young though, probably only seventeen years of age. Flaming red hair and petrified emerald eyes. Torches surrounding the platform flickered and wavered against the dragon's wing-created-wind. The girl's eyes bulged and soon the ear piercing torturous sound of her scream rang through the air.

The dragon's razor sharp claws dug into the old wooden platform, stopping its body's motion. The wood groaned and protested beneath his weight. The dragon rolled his eyes. Humans really underestimated his weight and size when they had built the altar. The sacrificial woman had passed out, and she was slumping against the ropes. They dug into her tender, pale flesh.

Shifting his weight carefully, the dragon tried not to wave his tale which caused the platform to creak relentlessly. He hovered on three legs, lifted up the fourth, and swiped the rope with it, catching the girl's tiny frame before she hit the hard wood.

The dragon shifted the girl's body so that he could grip her tight enough but without causing any harm. The dragon wings lifted its body twenty feet into the air with a single flap. He lofted himself away swiftly through the air as the sun began to rise; he needed to be back to his home before the sun rose. His grey green scales would stick out like a sore thumb against the blue background.

The girl's body dangled helplessly from between the dragons talons as he flew. He pushed himself fast until finally the clearing beside the beach where he had left his things came into view. Swooping down low, the dragon arched himself backward so that he could land more with his hind legs than his front.

"Isn't she a pretty one," someone said from a seated position behind the dragon.

The dragon turned his head and nodded. "She is a stunning one. Quite young though, maybe we could trade her," His words were thickly laced with a heavy Latin accent, and he knew that the girl wouldn't understand if she was awake.

The dragon placed the girl down and strode toward the edge of the sand. The man stood from his spot and strut toward the dragon, wanting to check out the girl. He had left his clothing over there.

The massive beast ducked its head and curled its spine as the metamorphism took place. His body cracked and crumbled, shortened and changed. Within no time, he laid there stark naked, the man of his other half.

Standing up, he grabbed hold of his clothing, pulling them on piece by piece. The dawn was warmer now, yet the thick moisture from the earlier hours still held. Once dressed, he rejoined the other man.

One knelt before the girl, eyeing her. They would take her to the women's cottage; they would check her wounds, from the ropes she had been confined with. The girl's head twitched and her eyes fluttered opened as one of the men lifted her up.

She was confused, it was understandable. She did not understand. The dragon should have eaten her, not delivered her here.

Her eyes were as wide as saucers, and Victor began slowly, "You are ours now and you will never return to your home."

It was finally beginning to click. These men were the legendary shape shifters which her people feared. "Are you going to eat me?" she whimpered.

The alpha chuckled. "We might."

"Please don't kill me," she cried trying to scurry away.

An evil grin passed over the man's lips as Victor lifted the girl up. She kicked and screamed.

"Oh my god, my family," the girl cried out as the man chuckled evilly.

"Do not worry. They have given you and next month… another." The girl's scream echoed through the jungle, but nobody would hear her. They were miles from her old village.

"Your screams are useless."

Chapter 6

The flight was longer than Miley had expected, and she struggled to stay awake as the plane landed on the main Galapagos Island.

"Ma'am," a woman's voice broke through her dreams.

Jumping slightly, Miley looked up to a stewardess staring down at her. "Ah…" Miley mumbled.

"The plane has landed and…" the stewardess began.

"Oh!" Miley said jumping up until she realized her seatbelt held her down. Her body slammed back into the chair. "Ouch," she groaned. "I'm sorry."

"It's alright, ma'am. It happens with a lot of people," she shrugged making her way for the baggage hold above Miley's head.

Miley unbuckled the seat belt and accepted her bag sheepishly from the woman. She could not believe she had fallen asleep in such a short time. She pushed herself out of the plane and through the corridor to the terminal. Unsure of what to do next, Miley slowed her pace and looked around nervously. She had never traveled outside of the United States, and she certainly hadn't travel alone.

Then she noticed him. He was a tall man with long dark hair dangling over his eyes. A thick black design spanned the skin across his left arm and disappeared beneath the shirt he wore. In his hands was a large piece of cardboard with 'Siegel Images" sprawled in a messy handwriting on it.

Gulping, Miley sucked in a deep breath. The man was scary in an 'I'll eat you alive' kind of way. She watched for a moment, while everyone who walked past avoided the man like the plague. It probably did not help that he was a foot taller or more than most of the people around here. Most people seemed to watch him out of the corners of their eyes, suspiciously, as they passed.

Miley took in another deep breath and let it out slowly as she nervously hugged her carry-on bag tightly into her stomach. She stepped toward the man, gulping again. The man still looked around over her head as she came closer.

"Um…excuse me," she murmured slightly.

"I'm not interested." He snorted and looked down. "Well, I'll make an exception for you babe." He smirked.

Miley's eyes widened in shock and she gulped backing up slightly. "Uh… I'm Miley, I'm…"

"Don't tell me," He drawled. "You want to go back to a hotel with me and shack…" He winked making her blush and shake her head furiously. This had been a horrible mistake.

"I'm so sorry. This is a mistake, tell the magazine I'll send someone else, but it might take a few months…" Miley muttered stumbling away from the man as his cocky grin faded quickly. He began to look at Miley with wide eyes.

He took in her look and groaned. Victor hadn't planned on a woman coming to explore the island. This could work either way; this could be good, causing the exposure of the McBride clan, or this could be bad… very bad.

Siegel Images had been known for their male photographers and for their lack of female influence. He was not quite sure of anything at the moment. Victor wondered if he could take her home with him and forget about ruining the other clan...

"You're here from the photo company?" he stuttered.

The woman before him blinked up with wide brown eyes. The kind of eyes that trapped a man, pulled him in, and did not release him. She had her chocolate brown hair pulled back into a messy bun; strands of the brown locks had fallen out of their placement, making him think she had ruffled it in her sleep.

Victor fought the urge to reach out to her as she brought her luscious plump bottom lip into her mouth and nibbled on it nervously. She was beautiful. This was a problem; he was beginning to wonder if she could do the job for them or not.

"Yeah... I ..." she shivered. "I'm sorry..." She looked so vulnerable and scared to be standing there, which could work for him.

"Oh, my goodness, I'm so sorry, madam. Please let's start over." He surged forward, quickly coming up with a plan. He could work with this. His alpha was counting on this to ruin the McBride clan.

Tossing the cardboard aside he held out his hand. "I'm Victor. I'm here to escort you to the island." He sighed when she did not take his hand. He tried again. "I'm so sorry. I seriously don't get out much," he apologized.

Shakily, Miley pushed her hand away from her death grip on her suitcase. He reminded her of a man that could be a bad boy, the kind she avoided with passion. He just rubbed her the wrong way. She held out her hand warily and giggled nervously before speaking. "I'm Miley Tanner." Her voice was weak and shy. She still had a small grin on her lips from his words, and Victor could see all the trouble she could cause.

"Miley Tanner." He smiled nodding his head. "Do you mind if I carry that for you?" he asked holding out his hand. He could be gentle if he wanted; he could be human if he wanted. It was just something he did not normally do.

"Breakable," Miley muttered clutching her carry-on tighter to her chest.

He nodded and grinned. "I'm sure I can manage," he mused.

Slowly relaxing her grip, Miley let Victor take her bag. "Do you have more luggage?" he asked.

"Yeah…" she drawled looking around for the baggage claim.

"This way then," he said walking them over toward the far side of the terminal building. A small turntable, which Miley had missed when she exited the plane, lined the wall.

Victor really did not travel in the area much. His clan stayed far away from the McBride clan, but he had arrived early enough to get a feel for the airport. He had even rented a boat for the occasion. Everything was perfect. The girl would do plenty of damage among the clan, and that just made him smile.

As they approached, Miley sighed remembering how horrible the turntables were at JFK. "It's a black and pink suitcase," she groaned thinking of how hard it was going to be to find.

"Of course it is." He nodded smugly, looked down, obviously taking in her outfit with a look of interest.

Miley could tell what his smug look was about when they approached the small turntable. It had been turned off and only held one bag, Miley's pink and black suitcase.

"I don't know, but I assume your bag is the only pink and black one left." He chuckled dryly.

A small squeak of embarrassment escaped Miley's lips. Victor reached forward and grabbed the bag without another word, setting it down on the floor and hooking her carry-on bag on top. "Well, are you ready?" he asked.

Miley bit her lip and nodded. She followed closely behind as the people before Victor parted.

"Oh, my gosh…" Miley heard someone mumble as they passed. Her head spun around, but the person had snapped their mouth shut. When she turned back around she noticed Victor glaring at the person and frowning.

"What was that about?" Miley asked.

Victor's features changed from stern to soft and relaxed. "Oh… it's ah nothing. Don't listen to any of them," he said, hoping the girl wouldn't listen, hoping someone wouldn't stop her from leaving with him. People here could tell he was different, and they were afraid of him, but Victor wasn't going to let that stop him from finishing the mission.

They made it to the front of the building within minutes. The terminal Miley had landed at must have been one of the smallest among the buildings here. It seemed strange because outside was a busy bustling world.

The first thing that hit her, when they exited, was the heat. Miley groaned.

"What?" Victor asked.

"It's hot here," she muttered.

Victor let out a small chuckle, and held the car door open for her as she climbed in. "We have a half an hour drive to the dock," he told her as he started the car. "And we have air conditioning." He grinned.

She nodded. "Okay."

Miley tried to make small talk as they drove, but mostly it failed miserably. Luckily, Victor turned the radio on low to relieve some of the tension.

"Finally," Victor murmured and Miley grinned. "We're here." He turned toward her with a small smile. "I hope you don't mind boats."

Miley shrugged as she pushed the door open and looked toward the dock. A ferry sat tied to a large dock while a smaller motor boat sat docked on the other side. Well, at least it's a ferry, she thought to herself. When Victor walked up to the small motorboat, Miley nearly choked on air.

"Miss Tanner…" Victor asked.

Miley nodded stiffly before making herself walk toward the boat. Victor held out his hand to her, and Miley gratefully accepted it as she nearly toppled head-over-heels into the boat. Her flip flop sandals did not seem to like the slick edge and flooring of the boat.

"Thank you," Miley murmured taking her hand back quickly before looking back up at Victor in horror.

"I'm sorry but this is part of our policy," Victor said holding up a blindfold.

Miley scrambled back, gripping the edges of the boat; shaking her head adamantly, she refused. "I don't… I… I can't… No," she argued.

"Miss Tanner, if you would please take a seat… I promise I will stay on the far side of the boat, but this is our policy." Victor tried to calm her nerves.

Anxiety and nervousness filled Miley, but she slowly sat down. Shakily, she lifted her hand up and accepted the blindfold, sliding it over her eyes.

"Thank you," Victor whispered. This was going to be too easy. "Just relax and enjoy the ride."

Chapter 7

"Miss Tanner" Victor's voice rang out to Miley as the boat began to shift.

"Call me Miley," she told him turning her head up toward the sound of his voice.

"Miley," he said. "We have arrived. You may take off the blindfold," he said. Miley could tell he had a slight grin on his lips. She could hear it in his words and when she pulled the blindfold off eagerly, she confirmed it with her own eyes.

"Wow," she breathed taking in the surroundings. Tall stalked trees were in small clusters near the shore. Among the vast expanse of white sand, sea lions bathed in the sun. The boat docked and Victor stepped up onto a wooden surface, tugging the boat by rope to its edge.

"Miley?" he said holding out his hand to her once again. Miley reached out grasping Victor's hand tightly while he pulled her up to the wooden dock. She walked forward, mesmerized by her surroundings while Victor pulled the luggage and supplies from the boat. Miley could hear birds chirping, animals cooing, and the trees swaying while the water lapped against the shore.

There were no signs of human encroachment here besides the dock, and she liked it. Simply, serene, and beautiful.

"It's amazing, isn't it?" Victor said walking up beside Miley.

"Yeah it is," she breathed. That's when she noticed a small, strange-looking golf cart parked beside the dock, and a boat chained to the opposite side of the tree. Cocking her eyebrow slightly, she was curious as to why they seemed so strange there.

"We will be making camp here for the night," Victor said.

"That's fine," she assured. She bent down and tugged her shoes off so she wouldn't tumble through the sand. Victor let out a low whistle and Miley stiffened upright, turning to look back at him. He stood agape but did not answer when she asked, "What did I miss?"

With a simple shrug, Miley continued, "I can't believe I got the privilege of capturing images of this place," she told him looking up into Victor's mossy green eyes for the first time. They were almost unreal. She could not compare the color of his eyes to anything except the mossy green seaweed of the ocean.

"My family found this island, and we just had to share it with the world." He lied. "I think our tent would be good over here," he told her finally.

Miley looked over at Victor wide-eyed. "We can't share a tent," shehuffed.

Victor's broad smile grew larger. "Well, as much as I would love to share the tent with a beautiful woman like you darlin', I am going to sleep out here on the sand." He chuckled as Miley sighed in relief.

Victor had set up the tent quickly. He pushed a pillow and sleeping bag inside before he turned toward Miley. "Well, goodnight. I'll see you in the morning."

"Goodnight, Victor." Miley smiled softly as she slid inside the tent and zipped it closed.

Chapter 8

While Miley slept, Victor dumped the remaining luggage and supplies onto the dock. He was careful not to make a sound as he climbed into the boat. Grabbing the ores, he rowed the boat out into the ocean. When he was far enough away to turn on the motor, he saw the tent shake; he simply smiled.

"Hey!" Miley screamed. "You can't leave me here!"

Victor felt compelled to answer back. "I'll be back in a week."

"NO!" Miley screamed over the sound of the motor. Victor just waved. Turning his head; he allowed the boat to disappear from the girl's view.

Tears fell from Miley's eyes. Frantically wiping them away, she sighed. The torch which Victor had lit earlier was beginning to fade, and the darkness was beginning to consume her.

Miley screamed "AH!!" then kicked the sand. She did not know what else to do in her tired and groggy state so Miley crawled back into the tent. She would figure out what to do in the morning.

When dawn finally came, Miley awoke to the sound of the ocean lapping at the shore and birds singing their love songs. She reached up and unzipped the tent. Sliding out, she stretched. "I can't believe that idiot left me here," she growled to herself.

She decided the best thing to do was to check out the items which Victor had left for her. Miley yawned as she padded her way through the sand. The supplies Victor had left at least held a bag of apples, which caused Miley to stop searching. She grabbed an apple and bit into it.

She figured since she was stuck here she would take the photos, which she needed, and pray Victor came back for her. Shoving her mp3 player's ear buds into her ears and grabbing her camera, Miley wandered off.

She decided the first pictures she would take were of the golf cart thing and the boat, neither of which she would be able to use. They were chained to the tree. Oviously somebody did not want them used.

Her camera clicked, and once Miley was satisfied with those, she decided to wander down the shoreline. It was beautiful here. She captured photos of the ocean, sea lions on the sand, and even parts of the reef.

After a while, Miley came to a river which flowed down into the ocean. Looking up the stream she wondered, if she stayed by the river… would she be able to find her way back to the shoreline?

Deciding that was exactly what she would do, Miley grabbed hold of a couple of sticks and created an arrow marking which way to turn once she returned to the sand. Then she took her chances and stepped into the brush.

The scenery was amazing. Miley took pictures of exotic birds, giant tortoises, lizards, and even multi-colored crabs crawling around. She was beginning to turn back around, when she heard a noise.

Pausing, Miley looked out into the jungle canopy trying to catch a glimpse of what was inside. Tentatively, she took a step but then thought better of it and continued back down the river to the shoreline. Dusk was coming, and she needed to find the campsite before the sun went down. She needed to make a fire, find food, even if it was within the supplies, and got ready for bed.

As she finally stumbled onto the sandy shoreline, Miley felt relieved. Quickly, she jogged back down the beach to her campsite and began her nightly preparations.

Chapter 9

Knocking on the wooden door of Diesel's office, Grant prepared for conflict. "Who is it?" Diesel snapped. He did not like to be disturbed this late at night.

"Alpha, its Grant," Grant called to his alpha from the far side of the door.

"What do you want?" Diesel demanded.

"May I come in?" Grant asked cautiously. Jessica allowed him in the house, but she did not authorize anyone into the alpha's office.

"Come in, come in." Diesel grunted.

Grant pushed the door open and stepped inside quickly. Letting out an impatient sigh, Grant spoke. "Alpha, a woman was spotted by the river today," he rushed.

"WHAT?!" Diesel asked.

"Yes, sir, I believe she is human. The clan member who spotted her was too afraid to approach. He said he hadn't ever seen her before," Grant urged.

"Set out a perimeter search. I want to know where she is now. We will have a meeting to alert the clan," Diesel said with authority.

"Yes, alpha." Grant nodded.

Grant stepped from the office and began to speak with the night staff. Diesel pushed from his chair then followed him out.

"Set out perimeter monitors guarding the village. We don't know what she is doing here. I want to know where she is, and I want her watched. If the girl causes trouble, I'll intervene," Diesel told him then continued to his library.

It had been years since they had visitors on their island. Main island residence never visited here. They were too afraid of the consequences.

It was nearly dark when Diesel brought the McBride clan to order in the meeting room of his home. It was the biggest home on the village and was where every clan member was welcomed if there was a threat.

"Hello, everyone," he called above murmuring voices.

The room fell silent. The clan members' respect was impeccable. "I have called this meeting tonight because a stranger has been spotted wandering around by the river."

Murmurs and chatter began and he continued. "Currently, we are assessing the threat. I would like to have everyone be aware of things around them. Do not talk to anyone you don't know! Do not get caught shifting! I am putting a ban on shifting within the outer limits. Only shifting within the village and designated safe zones until further notice. When we have found the person… she will be watched. If necessary we will take her into custody and question her. But until then, everyone be safe," Diesel told his clan.

After the meeting, Diesel released everyone to their homes. Already being late, he walked up to Grant, yawning. "I am going to bed. If there is any urgent news, make sure I am woken," he told him.

Chapter 10

The perimeter guards shifted into their beautiful cryptic beasts. One after another, creatures appeared where men once stood, each brandishing a different beautiful color; there was a creature for nearly every color of the rainbow, but these were warriors. They wore stern cold looks.

Their features weren't important to them, but their strength, stealth, and concentration were key. "Do not get seen!" the guard leader called out.

"Yes, sir!" The warriors answered.

"Our alpha, Diesel, has asked us to search the perimeter and scout for a woman. They are suspecting her to be human." A tall golden colored dragon spoke. He was the leader of the perimeter patrol group.

"Sir." A smaller yellow and golden colored dragon stepped forward.

"Yes, Derek?" the leader asked.

Derek cleared his throat and shifted his weight as he stood slightly taller. "Do we leave in teams?"

"Well, son," The leader began to reply with a tone which signified that he would have held a proud smile. Derek was his prodigy, his son, the one who would soon take over his own patrol party. "That's a good idea. Look after one another. The woman has posed no threat so far. Keep your distance. We are only scouting for where she is staying."

When the small speech was concluded, the beasts took flight while others wandered the forest. They had excellent night vision, and would use the night to their advantage.

Throughout the night, eight of the magnificent creatures combed the island. They had searched a third of the land by the time morning came and still hadn't found her campsite.

Assembling in the small clearing once again, they reported their findings to the leader. "We found no signs of her, sir."

"We will keep the clan on high alert. If anyone spots her, I want to know immediately." The leader said, sighing.

Their alpha wouldn't appreciate this at all. He might even be furious, but there was nothing the patrols could do if they could not find the woman.

Chapter 11

The next day, Miley crawled out from her tent; once again, birds alerted her of the morning. She changed her clothing, putting on a bikini and a simple spring dress. Miley searched through the supplies Victor had left her and sighed.

"Well, at least he left me some food and water," she groaned. She would definitely complain to the magazine company about their shady guide.

She combed the photos in her camera and decided that she really had to start to break through the outer shell of the island and explore the jungle. She had concluded this was a pretty big island and that she would probably get many complaints if she only showed up with pictures of animals and sand.

After eating an apple and a breakfast bar, Miley grabbed hold of a backpack and wandered over to the tent. Unzipping the tent, Miley dumped everything onto her sleeping bag. Then meticulously, Miley packed the items, which she thought would be necessary to carry along with her. She packed some food and water bottles, a pad of paper and pencils, her solar charging dock for her camera, her mp3 player, and her knife; along with anything else that seemed important.

Miley slipped on a pair of sandals, and then lopped the backpack over her back and the camera strap over her neck; she let out a breath and walked straight for the trees.

Miley pushed and shoved at the brush and walked straight into the canopy. After what seemed like forever of huffing into the trees, Miley began to wonder how bad of an idea this really was.

She could not see a path back in any direction, and a tear escaped her eyes. Miley had walked for hours. There was nothing more she could do but continue on her aimless mission through the trees, hoping to eventually emerge on the shore somewhere.

Thankfully, after another few miles, Miley had come into a clearing. It was a good place to rest; a section that was bare and dry. She pulled the backpack off her back and set it down on a rock. Her stomach rumbled and, now that she was lost, she really did not know if she should eat or ration what she had.

Sighing, Miley decided that she needed to eat a bit and drink some. She pulled one of the water bottles from her backpack and cracked it open. Tipping her head back slightly and gulping down a small bit, Miley sighed. Why had she been so stupid to wander into the canopy without the help of a gps marker to get back to the shoreline, or a map, or …Well… it was an uncharted, undocumented, unexplored island she reminded herself.

Tears flowed freely now down Miley's cheeks. Would she ever get home again? Would she starve to death on this island, or would she die of dehydration?

Darkness began to fall and Miley shivered slightly. How stupid had she been to not bring warmer clothing? She hadn't brought a sweater, no jeans, and nope… not even a blanket.

Searching for something that she could use to start a fire with, Miley whimpered when she came up short. She hated her life. Why had she decided to go on this stupid trip anyway?

Her parents would be so ashamed that their daughter was so stupid. They had never encouraged her love of photography. They had wanted her to do something better in their opinion, like marry Leon, who did not like her love for photography either.

When Miley refused his proposal, after finding him in bed naked with her sister… she rebelled and flew out to New York, taking the job at Siegel on a whim. Her parents wouldn't release her trust fund until she turned twenty-one and returned home or married the man of their choice. Now, she seriously contemplated her sanity.

So…contemplating her sanity, cold, afraid, and alone, Miley curled into a ball and covered herself with a few big leaves she had pulled from the lowest branches of trees that she could find.

Chapter 12

The next night, the perimeter patrol set out again. They set out as soon as the night would cover them from sight. Searching by foot did not really get them far, so instead of wasting their energy in that way, the group rested and waited until it was dark once again.

"This time I want to have the focus on the shore line. That is where we should have started. I want each group to fly out in their specified direction toward the ocean. We will fly around in each direction until the entire shore line is covered. If you do not spot anything by the time you meet up with another dragon, take to the inner island, and focus on the parts of the island which we haven't covered yet." the leader told his patrollers.

"Yes, sir!" the dragon patrollers barked back.

They removed their articles of clothing and shifted with ease, letting the night's crisp air waft over them as they did so.

The patrollers had met in the village center tonight, each having said goodnight to their families. Once their partners had shifted, the teams headed out. The village sounded like a massive wind tunnel as a multitude of dragons took flight flapping their massive wings and lifting their colorful bodies into the night air. A chuff-like sound from their leader alerted them to take their leave of the village in search of the woman.

Derek, the young patrol leader's son and his partner, Max, a massive creamy orange dragon took off to the east while two others headed to the north, south, and west. Derek and Max were usually partners, best friends, yet both were focused and strict warriors.

Together the two flew, their wings nearly touching as they swept through the sky. Each with their heads tilted downward searching for a sign that a visitor was below. Once they reached the beach, they turned right flying toward the next group's location.

Max's chuff alerted Derek. Derek turned his head toward his friend with a quick nod; the two dragons dropped to the ground. They had found a camp.

"I'll shift and search the tent," Derek whispered to his partner.

Max nodded and stood guard while Derek shifted and pulled on a pair of shorts he had tucked in a pack around his calf. It was specially made to expand with the growth of a dragon's leg.

Derek carefully stalked forward. He knew Max had his back and would make sure that nobody snuck up on him. The camp site seemed to be abandoned. Nodding his head over the tent, Max suggested Derek check the inside. Slowly, Derek reached for the zipper.

The zzzzzziiiiiiiiiiiippppppppppp of the zipper was like the sound of fingernails on a chalk board. It ripped through the night, and Derek cringed. He could not be any quieter. Yet, when he pulled open the tent's flap, he was surprised not to find someone within.

"It's empty," he called over to Max.

Max cocked his head. "Really?" he asked.

"Yeah," Derek said breathily as he stepped inside. Calling out again, "and it's cold. Nobody's been here in a while," he told Max as he felt the sleeping bag and stepped out.

Zipping the tent back up, both guys wondered where the woman could be. "It's definitely a human girl. The stuff is a female's for sure, and the bed's scent is human," Derek said.

"Well, should we go looking for the girl or should we go back and alert the alpha?" Max asked.

"I'll look for the girl. You go back and update the alpha, then see if he would mind if you come out and join in the search," Derek said.

"I don't know, Derek… You don't know what the human's capable of, she could be dangerous," Max told his friend sincerely.

"Max." Derek shook his head. "I can easily shift and take out any threat. Besides, it's just a human girl. I'm sure she's like any other," Derek assured.

Derek watched as his friend took to the sky. Then, letting his sense of smell guide him, Derek sucked in a deep breath and took to the jungle.

Chapter 13

Shifting as he landed, Max tugged on a pair of shorts and hurried toward the alpha's house. Dawn was coming and he was still anxious about his friend's decision. Yet, Derek was his superior, and Max followed orders to a tee.

He stepped up to the alpha's home and knocked. Footprints on the other side of the door quickly alerted Max that someone was coming to answer him. He sucked in a breath and stood tall, confident.

"Ah… Max." Jessica smiled; she was the head of the staff at the alpha's home and held the position proudly. If she did not want to let a clan member in … they did not come in.

"Jessica," Max said with urgency. "I need to speak to the alpha," he told her.

"Oh, of course, I assume you have news of the patrols?" she questioned as she held open the door allowing Max to walk in.

"Yes, ma'am," he told her.

"Well, you know the way." Jessica smiled. It wasn't uncommon for a patroller to come to the alpha's house; they were usual guests for dinners and meetings, so it was certain that Max would know the way.

"Thank you," Max said as he continued through the house. Walking the hall until he came to Diesel's door, Max did not need to knock, the door was wide open.

"Ah. Max, news of the patrol?" Diesel asked sitting up slightly.

"Yes, alpha," Max replied.

"Well, go ahead." Diesel urged.

"Derek and I found a campsite. The bedding was cold, and it seemed to be vacant for a while."

"Well, then." Diesel grinned. The threat was over then. A campsite cleanup wasn't that bad.

"It is definitely a human, and all the items suggest the human is a woman. Derek set into the jungle to track her, while I returned to inform you." Max rushed to say.

"Oh" Diesel replied. Taking in the man's anxious behavior, Diesel raised an eyebrow "And I am sure you are anxious to assist in the search?"

"Yes, alpha." Max shifted his position.

"Thank you for the update. Please inform me if you find the woman," Diesel told him. "Now go ahead and meet up with your partner."

Max sighed in relief before swiftly turning and making his way down the hall. As he exited the house, Max was already stripping his shorts, folding it into his calf pack, and shifting.

Warrior dragons were teamed together and linked together through magic. Max's feather light wings flapped, lofting himself up into the air. Without hast, he followed his connection, quickly making his way to his partner's side. He did not expect for Derek to be so close.

Chapter 14

Derek could feel the connection of his patrol partner as he neared, so he halted his pace. He could tell the human was close now; her scent was all over the clearing where the dragons had gathered just days before.

Max dropped through the jungle canopy, his beast's size did not affect his descent. It was nearly as silent as a whisper as he landed beside his patrol partner. He shifted and pulled on his shorts. "Wow… I can smell the human all over here." Max stiffened.

"Yeah, she's in the clearing," Derek said confidently.

The two men slowly stalked forward. The daylight was brighter now. Off to the center of the clearing, sitting on a rock was a back pack. "Look," Derek whispered.

Then they saw her. She was a slight form curled up beneath leaves and shivering terribly. Derek cocked his head slightly. The girl obviously was human, her scent filled him and it was foreign, yet intriguing.

Max sighed as he leaned down. He was wary of the human. Unlike Derek and many of the guards, the alpha, and beta as well, Max had never traveled to the main land. He had never met a human besides the ones which the dragon shifters had mated too; all of which were tamed, he figured.

Slowly reaching out his hand, he ran it along the girl's cheek. "She's freezing." He sighed looking up at Derek.

Knowing his friend was unsure and unknowing of anything human, Derek stepped forward. He knew human's body temperature was lower, much lower than that of a dragon. He reached down, placing the back side of his hand against her cheek. "She's freezing," Derek affirmed with slight shock. "She's a lot colder than she should be." He quickly shoved away the leaves covering her body and instantly knew why she was cold. The girl was practically naked. Yes, she had clothing, but not enough for the cool night. Sighing he shoved his arm beneath the girl's thighs and the other behind her back and head.

"What are you doing?!" Max hissed.

"She's cold," he told Max. "I need to warm her. Build a fire. We're staying for a while," Derek told Max.

Max's eyes were wide, but he followed his friend's demand. Quickly piling up the leaves the girl had been wrapped up in and a few sticks, in a makeshift pit, Max waved his hand over the materials. Sparks quickly ignited the branches and fire soon followed.

The girl was either a deep sleeper or too cold to be responsive. Derek quickly strode over to Max's fire and curled himself onto the grassy ground, tucking the girl into his body and resting her head against his bare chest.

After nearly half an hour, the girl began to wiggle. She was trying to get more comfortable obviously. Pulling her back into his chest to keep the girl warm, Derek chuckled slightly.

Max watched as his friend cared for the human. He wasn't sure how Derek knew so much about humans, but he seemed to know just what the girl had needed. The girl murmured, rubbing her face into Derek's chest before she rubbed her hand across it.

"What the?!" she suddenly screeched, surprising Derek and Max. The girl quickly tried to scramble from Derek's arms, but he gripped tighter. Frightened, the girl's eyes went wide and she screamed.

Chapter 15

"Hey. Calm down, no screaming, please," Derek complained.

"Who are you?" the girl cried pushing against Derek's chest. "Let go of me!"

"Well, hello to you too. I am Derek, and this is my friend, Max. What's your name?" Derek asked.

The girl pushed harder. Derek sighed, finally allowing the girl to slip from his grasp, but not allowing her to tumble into the fire pit. "Watch out for the fire," he told her.

Max observed as the girl eyed them. Her eyes flit over to the fire pit then back to the men as she scrambled across the clearing to the rock which held her bag.

Derek and Max stood. Neither realized how intimidating they were to this woman until, with widened eyes, she scrambled around to the far side of the rock and screamed "Stay away."

"Take it easy." Max offered.

"We're here to help you," Derek said slowly holding out his hand as if he was calling her back to him. "Now… what's your name?"

Slowly, the girl began to speak, "Miley."

"Well, Miley, why don't you come back to the fire, and once you're warm enough, we will head back to our village."

Miley's brows furrowed in confusion, and she cocked her head slightly as she grasped her bag and slowly began to drag it toward the fire. "Village?" Miley repeated.

Max nodded. "We live here."

Miley did not know exactly if she believed them. She had been told that the island was uninhabited.

She made her way to the fire and curled her knees into her chest. She shivered slightly. Max sat down cross-legged on the opposite side of the fire observing the woman while Derek shook his head. Max watched as his friend walked right up to the human, sat down, and pulled her into his lap. Even though Miley protested, Derek held firm. "I run warmer than you do. So… use my heat."

When the sun finally came up and it was warmer outside, the trio made their way through the jungle canopy.

"Where have you been? We've been …" Jonah, the patrol leader and Derek's father, shouted. His words died in his mouth as he watched the small figure of a woman shiver between Derek and Max.

"We found the woman." Derek shrugged.

Jonah's eyes were wide, and he looked fiercely back toward the woman. "And you brought her here?" Jonah howled.

"What else were we to do with her? She was cold and lost, freezing to death in the training field." Max snorted. He had watched the interactions of Derek and Miley and was beginning to like her. She seemed so much different than what he had always thought about humans.

Jonah also snorted, turned on his heels and stomp away.

"We'll take you to our chief…" Derek said and chuckled slightly.

"Chief?" Max asked, questioning the word. He obviously did not catch on.

"Diesel," Derek replied.

Miley swallowed a lump in her throat as they approached the edge of the village. "This is your village?" she whispered quietly.

Buildings began to come into view within a semi cleared out area. Miley smiled at the simplicity. This was where the village started.

Miley really did not know what she was expecting when the two guys told her they would take her to their village, but this was not quite it. The beautifully displayed homes had thatch roves. A medium sized windmill stood proudly in the center of the small village. They came to a stop before a large beautiful structure.

"Yeah," Derek answered.

"Huh…"

"This is our village chief's home.…" Max said.

"You will be respectful and silent unless spoken too," Derek said firmly, which slightly scared Miley. He seemed so much more different now that, if it had been an hour earlier, she would have simply run away.

Miley nodded her head but did not reply. Derek held up his hand and knocked on the front door of the home.

Chapter 16

Miley nervously bounced from foot to foot. She wasn't quite sure she was ready for this. Derek and Max had treated her well while they were with her and she probably would have froze if they did not come to her aid, but was this really a safe place to be right now?

She had been told that the island was uninhabited and unexplored. Obviously, the island was neither. Why were these people so secretive that nobody knew they were here?

With Derek on one side focused thoroughly on the door before him, and Max concentrating on something that wasn't her, Miley slowly stepped back. One step at a time and within moments she was in her own space and running. The two men had been so focused on what they were doing and on speaking to each other that they almost made it too easy for her to escape.

It worked! She had nearly shouted it but thought better. Hoisting her bag up tighter on her shoulder, and thankful that Max and Derek had let her have it back, she raced toward the edge of the village.

Once inside the tree line, she did not stop. Miley pushed harder, further into the trees. They had passed the river which she had once walked up, and she knew it would lead her to the shoreline where she could find her camp.

She hadn't told the two men that she was camping on the beach and for that she was immensely thankful. Though, she felt bad for the men and hoped that they did not get in trouble for anything.

Every little crack of sticks beneath her feet or wave of leaves from birds, made Miley nervous. Would they come after her? No, they wouldn't. She was a grown woman, and she could take care of herself. She doubted that Max and Derek would necessarily be the kind of chivalrous men who came tramping through the woods to find her.

Once her bare feet, yes bare, hit the water of the small river, Miley paused for a sigh of relief, thinking that she was going to be safe.

That was until she heard something coming from behind her. "Where did she go?" asked the voice of a man she did not recognize.

"I don't know, Derek probably scared her off." Max complained.

Miley sucked in a deep breath and took off running again. The men sounded as if they had been a ways away, but she did not want to stick around and have them stumble upon her.

Her lungs burned and her body ached but she continued. She did not have a choice; for some reason she did not want to go back to that village. Well, at least not with those men. She would maybe spy on the village later on since she had noticed a large 'y' in the river which she could easily find to point out the turn where she could take the path back to the village.

She wanted to know these people more before she was trapped in a close confined area with them. The strange way Derek and Max interacted with her made her curious. Max had looked at her as if she was infected and would tear his head off at any second, while Derek was strange with his touchy-gotta-hold-onto-you type weirdness. What was with that "I run warmer than you" thing he had said.

Pushing harder, Miley was running faster than she ever had in her life. She ran down the water on the side of the small river bank. For some reason, she knew if they were to track her, a dog would lose the scent of her in the water, though she doubted they had dogs on the island.

When Miley finally burst onto the beach, she breathed a heavy sigh of relief. The sign she had made on the ground in the sand was the most beautiful sight she had ever seen but now she was going to destroy it.

Picking up the pieces of the arrow, she tossed them all into the trees then brushed it away with her foot as she back tracked over to the ocean's edge. There she once again ran within the edge of the water.

When Miley finally reached her camp site, she could tell that someone had looked around. There were tracks from shoes, too large to be her tiny feet, and strange tracks which scared her some.

The massive footprints of some creature made her afraid to do anything other than crawl into her tent and cry. The print was well over five times the size of her foot and had marks that dug into the ground at the tips, maybe claws. It looked like a lizard's print but much larger.

She raked her brain trying to figure out if she had ever heard of any giant lizards other than the Komodo Dragon, which was the biggest she could think of, but she knew that this one was much bigger. Maybe if she was lucky it would be the tracks of a giant vegetarian bird or something less threatening than a giant lizard.

With each passing thought, Miley grew more tired. The past few hours were an emotional roller coaster, and she was exhausted. After curling tighter into her sleeping bag, Miley slowly slipped asleep.

Chapter 17

Miley may have been warm and snuggled up sleeping soundly within her tent, but she wasn't quite as alone as she thought she was. Miley knew the men she had run from would find her eventually.

When she awoke, it was dimly lit inside the tent and she wondered if it was still the same day she had run from the men. The air was warm today, and she felt a slight breeze blow through her long hair as she looked out at the ocean. She wondered when someone would come and rescue her and take her back home to the life she had - not really the life she loved but the one she lived, at least.

Stepping from the confines of the tent onto the warmth of the sand, Miley stretched up and yawned. She loved the beauty of this island. It was so much more beautiful than the concrete that surrounded her every day at home.

She wandered over to the water and dipped her feet into the coolness of the ocean, wondering how long it would be before that idiot came back for her. She could not believe he had left her in the first place.

Those thoughts caused her anger to boil over, and Miley let out a frustrated "Gah!" scream. She kicked viciously at the water and scoffed as she stomped back and forth.

What about the boat… she began to wonder. Knowing now that there were people on this island explained a lot about what she was confused about at first. It was now obvious why there was a boat and a four wheeler chained up. It was obvious why there was a dock here…

How could she have been so stupid? The entire trip had to be a rouse for something. It had to be something.

Maybe the man had been trying to get the people on this island mad; that made her nervous.

Miley was hungry. It had been a long time since she had eaten and now that her frustrations were out and kicked into the water, she figured she might as well sit down and enjoy something to eat.

When she got back over to the supplies, Miley began to scrounge inside. What was there left to eat? She grabbed a water bottle, cracked it open and swigged it, then began looking again. She decided a breakfast bar and an apple would be satisfying enough for right now.

Standing up, Miley walked back over to the tent and curled her legs beneath her, sitting Indian style watching out toward the ocean. She munched greedily upon the bar first as she watched the waters lap at the sand.

Would they find her? If so, what would she do if they were as aggressive as she was worried about? "I'll just have to prepare," Miley said to herself firmly.

She felt so alone here, but she wasn't going to dwell on it. Before she set out for her morning photo shoot, Miley packed up the things. She made sure to pack up as much of the things as she could. The tent was easy, being a simple pop-up tent, while the heavier things might have to be left behind.

Unsure of where she really was going to go, Miley set off along the shore line for a while. She knew the water would eventually wash away her footsteps and that's exactly what she was counting on.

"Uhg," shegrunted as she hoisted the heavy bags upon her shoulders higher.

A loud crack startled her, and Miley cursed as her bag dropped into the water. "Damn it!" she hissed and turned sharply toward the noise. She glared into the edge of the tree line where a coconut had fallen and hit a rock. Since her bag was already wet, she simply kicked it slightly higher onto the beach and stomped angrily over to the obnoxious fruit.

Since the coconut had fallen down and disturbed her, she was going to eat it. An evil grin grew on Miley's lips, and she grabbed harshly at the fuzzy thing. If it was ripe enough, she could have coconut milk. If not, she would be plenty happy eating the yummy fruit inside. Either way, she glared at it harshly then began to look around again. If there were more of coconuts, she might just take them too.

A few coconuts littered the ground, and Miley was tired from all the walking so she decided to stay for lunch. Maybe she would make this her new campsite, though she thought it would be better if she had a more secretive spot. She was probably a few miles from the original campsite and could not see it at all after she had passed the first turn of the island.

Miley set the coconut, that she was angry at, her first victim, down on the sand and quickly returned to her water soaked bag. There were trees here which were angular, and she could dry some things on them. So, doing just that, Miley pulled out the tent and set it up, quickly placing her dry things inside.

Those items which were wet, Miley slung over the lowest branches and trunks of curved trees. She looked up at the sky and tried to gage the time. Ironically enough, her watch had given out the other day, when she was sleeping in the meadow.

By the rumble of her stomach and the sun's height in the sky, she figured it was around noon. Miley busied herself finding a few pieces of firewood which she figured she would need if she was going to eat anything warm, then she curled into the warmth of the sand, preparing for something to eat.

First up, the infuriating coconut. It really was an ugly beast of a fruit and because it so rudely scared her, it deserved to be eaten.

Now, how to open it? She thought to herself as she searched around for something sharp. Thankful enough, Miley had come across a knife which had been within the packed materials and hoped it would work well enough.

The coconut was hard. She jabbed at it with all her might and still the knife did not even scrape its surface. Groaning, Miley looked around for a better option.

A short distance from her new campsite, a rock proved that this was the perfect spot for Miley to be staying. The site was surrounded by high sharp pointed rocks. A small cove of water off to the back side made her curious about if fish might trapped inside for an easy dinner.

The rock she chose was sharp edged and broke the coconut well. Luckily, the coconut was not yet fully liquefied, and she did not lose the nutritious contents.

Taking the knife from where she had angrily dropped it before, Miley began to cut off slices of the coconut and chew them greedily. It was like heaven in her mouth, especially with the hunger that was growing in her stomach.

When her stomach was full and her campsite set up to her liking, Miley pulled on her stuffed backpack and her camera, for a walk around the area. She was determined to find something worth her time here.

Chapter 18

Diesel was furious. The girl had obviously been up to something, or she wouldn't have run away. "Max, Derek, show me where that campsite is," Diesel demanded.

The clan's perimeter patrol had searched for a while and never had come up with the girl. They hadn't know quite where she had gone since her scent had disappeared. They were still searching when Diesel decided what he would do.

He would go after her himself. "Yes, alpha," Derek and Max answered.

The three men walked out into the central village area and Derek and Max turned to Diesel to ask, "Are we going to shift or walk?" Derek questioned.

"Walk. I don't want that woman catching us flying. During the day it would be too easy for her to see us," Diesel said.

Max and Derek nodded. "Her camp's over that way," Max said, pointing off toward the far distant shoreline.

"Okay then, let's go," Diesel said, stomping off in the direction.

They had been going through the trees in the general direction of the shore for a while now and Diesel was growing more and more annoyed.

"She's definitely human?" he questioned.

"Yes, alpha," Max said.

"She's a beautiful one at that." Derek grinned.

Diesel growled and turned his head slightly to glare at the man. "I don't want anyone getting too attached to her. She's going right into the cells until we find out why she's here," Diesel snapped.

"She seemed nice," Max said with a slight smile. He was remembering back to the field and when they had at least gotten her name from her.

"All you got was her name…" Diesel reminded the man. "She's up to something. I know it," he grumbled.

An hour's walk and they finally emerged on the beach. "Her camp was that way. Just to the right by a quarter hour walk from the river mouth," Derek told his alpha.

Diesel glanced over and nodded. When they arrived there, he would show the girl who's boss. Diesel stomped off toward the river mouth and then further toward where the prospective campsite was supposed to be.

"Gone," Derek and Max mouthed in a near whisper.

"Spread out and search for her. She could not have gone far. If she's off the island… bring her back! We need to know what she knows!" Diesel growled angrily.

Diesel stomped angrily down the sandy beach. Max and Derek went in different directions.

Diesel had followed the shoreline, stomping as he went. His pace was nearly a jog and he was determined to find the girl. When he finally rounded the corner of the shoreline and came across a new campsite, he had to practically chain the beast within him.

Sucking in deeply, Diesel could tell the girl wasn't here. The scent was stale, but she was definitely coming back. Why would she have taken the time to set up such an elaborate campsite if she wasn't?

Knowing that the girl would probably run again if she saw him, Diesel grunted with annoyance, then walked off into the tree line. He would hide out here. He would watch her every move until he felt it necessary to capture her.

Chapter 19

Miley had grown bored with wandering around the sandy area. She decided that she needed more pictures and so she had set out to find them. With her backpack on her back and her camera in hand, Miley walked toward the tall rocks.

There had been a lit area that she was sure lead to the other side, and sure enough, it did. When Miley had finished squeezing through the rocks, she was surprised to see a beautiful section of beach which seemed almost untouched. Quickly, she snapped off a few pictures.

It did not seem quite right only having pictures of the animals and life here. It seemed as if something was missing. Miley sighed and looked out into the ocean. The colors of the water changed and beneath the water was a reef, full of color and life.

Miley dropped her backpack on the ground and decided she would take a swim. She loaded up her camera into its waterproof case, slid off her dress and shoes, then trotted off toward the water.

When she was deep enough, Miley dove under the water and began snapping away pictures. There were corals and fish life she had never got to see so close before, and it was simply beautiful.

Miley had been swimming for nearly two hours, diving into the water and taking pictures then coming back up for air. She was so lost in thought that the sound of someone clearing their throat scared her.

"Well, look who we have here," Diesel announced.

Miley stayed silent but slowly turned around and looked at the man. "Get out of the water," he told her.

"I rather like it here," she said cooly.

"I want you out of the water," he growled.

"Did not your parents ever teach you, you don't always get what you want?" she retorted.

"Oh, but darling I do," Diesel said devilishly. He quickly turned his head to the side and nodded toward Miley. "Derek, Max, bring her back to the village. See you soon, princess."

Miley's eyes widened, for some reason she hadn't realized the other men were there. Her eyes had been transfixed on the big man before her. So, when Derek and Max stepped forward and were about to enter the water, she freaked.

Now, Miley watched as a woman opened the door smiling, but frowned as her eyes fell upon Miley herself. "Uh…" the woman muttered.

"Jess," Derek dragged. "Diesel, please."

"Uh…" Jessica replied.

"Jessica," Derek said sharply, snapping the woman out of her thoughts. "Now."

"Right, yes, just a moment," she mumbled. "I'll be right back," she said shutting the door behind her.

On the other side of the house, Jessica knocked urgently on Diesel's door. "What's with breaking down the door?" He huffed as he stood. It was such hard frantic pounding that the person on the other side did not even hear his 'Come in.'

Diesel yanked the door open and stared into the stressed face of Jessica. "What is it?" he grumbled.

"Alpha… woman… door…" she said anxiously.

"Speak clearer," he growled. "Now, what is it?" he asked again.

"Derek…" Jessica pointed.

"Grhhr," Diesel growled as he pushed past Jessica toward the direction she pointed. As he made his way to the door, he was grumbling, "Can't get good help anymore."

Diesel could smell the delicious yet foreign scent of the woman on the other side of the door and out of curiosity, he yanked it open. "Derek?" he questioned as the door opened.

Miley gasped at the sight before her. She hadn't expected such a big beastly handsome man to appear before her. The sun had shielded his looks from her earlier. He was handsome and massive, but that wasn't what caught her eye it was those eye, those violet eyes.

"Hello." Diesel snapped his eyes over to the woman with a crooked half smile. "It's nice to see you out of the water…" he said "I thought you said you rather enjoyed it there." Diesel teased.

Miley rolled her eyes. She had enjoyed the water and did not want to go with the men but as soon as Diesel ordered them to get her out and she tried to swim away, Max and Derek lunged.

The two had swam like snakes, fast and stealthy. One had grabbed her around the waist and yanked her up above the water. She did not stand a chance. As soon as they got close enough to shore to touch, the two men latched onto her wrists and hadn't let go since.

She was still dripping wet from her swim with sand clinging to her bare legs and feet. Her dress dangled from Max's arm and her bag over Derek's shoulder.

Diesel's eyes glazed over her body with lust, and he licked his lips slightly. "I rather like seeing you this way." He purred.

"Miley, this is Diesel, the leader of this island," Derek said.

"Come in…" Diesel muttered.

Miley shivered, the sun may have been up and it may have been warm in the ocean, but it was getting chilly with the wind whipping around, and her only wear was her bikini.

"You're cold?" Diesel asked in the tone of a comment more than a question.

"No…" Miley chattered.

"Yeah, she is," Derek admitted.

"I'm not cold," Miley stuttered again. She was looking down at the floorboards of the beautiful wood flooring, mildly afraid to look up at the towering man before her. She noticed how she was making a mess on the floor with sand and water drips and realized how annoyed the woman from earlier would be.

She heard a sigh before someone's hand clamped around her wrist. "Lying doesn't get you anywhere," the voice of Diesel said as he yanked her into his arms and sucked in her scent. "You're cold."

Miley was at a loss for words. She was quite small and insignificant within this big man's arms. He was, at the least, a foot and a half taller than her small frame and was very strong to boot.

"Jessica! Blanket now!" he shouted as he began to tow Miley through the house.

The large home was warmer than outside and surprisingly beautifully decorated. It was tropically decorated with minimalism as the key factor in its design.

Jessica, the woman from before, appeared with a thick comforter in her hands. "Alpha, this is all I could find on such short notice," she muttered as she raced toward them.

"Alpha?" Miley questioned.

"Max, please watch over Miss Miley here, while I talk with Derek," Diesel said sternly. "We'll be in my office."

With that, Diesel quickly wrapped a blanket around Miley's body and pushed her down into his couch before walking away and leaving her with Max quirking an eyebrow at her.

"What?" she squeaked.

"You like him?" he questioned.

"What? No!" She scoffed.

Max shrugged. "Okay," he said, knowing it was a lie.

"Jessica, could you bring Miley here a cup of your famous cocoa?" Max asked.

"Of course, Max," she beamed walking away.

Chapter 20

"She's definitely human." Diesel huffed as he shut the door to his office behind Derek.

"Yes. She is," Derek commented. "And you like her." He smirked.

"Don't be ridiculous!" Diesel snorted. "What is she doing here; did you get that out of her?"

"No," Derek replied. "She was pretty scared. We managed her name and that's about it. I told you that before, sir. But you're avoiding the subject, you like her."

"Well, then she's going to have to be locked up." Diesel growled as he stood up, once again ignoring the subject.

"Diesel, you can't…" Derek began to protest, but Diesel cut him short.

"I can and I will!" He roared. "I expect you to calm down before you regret your decision. I am alpha here!" Diesel snarled.

Derek hung his head. "Sorry, alpha," he murmured softly.

"Now… get my guards." Diesel snapped as he walked toward the door. "Tell Cain and Nick I want them here immediately!"

Diesel pulled the door open and stormed out. Stomping down the hallway and glaring at Max, who was just slightly too close to Miley. "What are you doing here?" He snarled.

Miley whimpered but did not look up at him.

"I said!" Diesel snarled out again. "What are you doing here?"

Miley sucked in a breath and swallowed the lump in her throat. "Your two boys forced me to walk back here," Miley muttered quietly.

She could tell the man was furious, but she was too afraid to do anything let alone say much. She wasn't stupid. She knew she was in danger.

Diesel roared. It was an inhuman sound, an ear piercing roar that Miley had never heard before and her hands automatically flew up to cover her ears. "Cain, Nick, get her out of here and don't let her out of your sight!"

With that, Miley was yanked upward and dragged away by the two burly men that appeared out of nowhere. "Where are we going?" She cried softly.

"You are our prisoner now," Nick shrugged, "you don't have the right to ask questions."

"She hasn't caused any problems!" Max took it as his turn to stand up for the woman.

"She doesn't answer questions. She's being detained. You should have left her in the jungle." Diesel growled.

"She would have died!" Max snapped.

"Max. You may be my little brother, but you are not the alpha. You are not my beta, you are not anything but a low member of this clan!" Diesel hissed. His hand flew out and gripped Max by the throat and hoisted him up against a wall.

"At least I have standards." Max choked out from beneath Diesel's iron grip. "At least, I wouldn't put her in a cell. I would treat her like a guest until she proved me wrong." Max croaked.

Diesel growled knowing Max was right and flung him across the room. "Cain!" he shouted.

Cain turned around leaving Nick holding Miley in the hallway. "Yes, alpha?" Cain asked.

"Bring her out back to the guest cabin. Stand guard and don't let her out of your sight." Diesel hissed.

Cain's eyebrows furrowed and he frowned. "Are you…" he began.

"Don't question me!" Diesel snapped abruptly cutting him off.

It had been a long time since Diesel had used his loving side of his heart. He was a firm leader, one who protected the clan fiercely, humans were only allowed here as sacrifices and they were never visitors. The ones here were mated off within the first week. He had no idea what this girl was doing to him, or why he thought she was so beautiful.

Chapter 21

Cain and Nick walked with Miley, she did not bother protesting, which they were grateful for. Cain understood human woman, as much as he could at least. His mate was a human sacrifice from the main island years ago.

He rather liked humans, his mate was caring, loving, and playful; the only quality she did not share with the dragons was the ability to shift into one. He had grown accustom to it over the years and even had a saddle type device fashioned for her so he could safely carry her around during flight.

Nick on the other hand was wary of the human. He only held tightly to her earlier because he was told to. She was so frail and small he was afraid he would break her. There had been stories…

The trio finally came to the back door of the alpha's house and opened it to the beauty of the back yard.

"Right this way." Cain said holding his hand out.

Miley stepped through followed closely behind by Cain and Nick. They walked down the stone path, which lead to a small cabin.

It was made with logs from the surrounding area, flowers and vines grew on it as if it was part of the natural scenery. Walking up on the porch Cain sighed, "This is where you will be staying."

"What have I done wrong?" Miley whimpered.

"Inside." Nick snapped. He wasn't afraid to yell at the woman. She may have been a woman but she was a human one.

Cain's head snapped over to Nick and he watched as the small woman nervously scooted though the door and away from Nick. "I heard you have a camp with some things…"

"Yes." Miley squeaked.

"I'll be sure to send someone to pack it up and bring it here. I'm sure you would like a change of clothing?" Cain said. He may have been a stern enforcer but he was still a man standing before a beautiful woman.

"Please." Miley whimpered.

Nick slammed the door. He stood on the small wooden deck glaring at his fellow guard. "What is wrong with you?" Nick hissed.

"What is wrong with you?" Cain replied.

"You are befriending a human?" Nick growled.

"Pish," Cain snorted. "I am being civil, she is scared…"

"HUMAN!" Nick growled.

"And…" Cain drawled. Nick took a menacing step forward. Cain raised an eyebrow curiously. "Seriously, you going to threaten me like that?"

"What part of human aren't you worried about…?" Nick snapped, he wouldn't fight Cain, he wouldn't win anyway.

"You're scared of her?" Cain chuckled; he eyed the man before him then added, "you are…"

"No!" Nick blurt out rubbing his hand through his hair and looking away.

"She's just a human Nick. Have you forgotten that I am mated to a human woman?" Cain questioned.

"A tamed one," Nick snorted.

"Tame? Yeah right… like you can tame a woman." Cain chuckled. "That woman in there" Cain pointed back toward the cabin, "Is more frail and vulnerable than you can imagine. She's terrified right now, far from home, and alone on an island where she's only mostly saw men. She probably did not even know this island had people on it!" Cain yelled. He stepped from the deck. "I am going to ask Max to go out and pack up her things. I'll be back in a few minutes. Don't do anything stupid."

Nick rolled his eyes, him do something stupid, ha! He looked around the small deck, spotting a swing on the far side, brought himself over to it and sat down.

"This is so stupid. Why do I have to sit here and babysit a human?" Nick snarled to himself after what seemed like an hour.

"Why would those two bring a dangerous human to our village? Now… I'm stuck watching her. What if she goes crazy and torches the place?" He hissed. Nick had been brewing in his anger the entire time that Cain was gone.

Miley walked around the small cabin, scared, hungry, and alone. There was a small kitchen and since she was locked inside she figured nobody would care or notice if she found something to eat.

Gingerly she padded over to the cupboards. On the counter sat a bowl of fruit, mostly strange looking ones, but some which she knew she would like. Strangely enough, when she pulled the cupboards open she found similar items that would be at a normal home, not a cabin in the middle of nowhere.

There were boxes of cereal and crackers, chips and granola bars. Nothing needed to be cooked and she was glad for that since she wasn't sure how she would cook without a stove, though strangely enough there was a small fridge.

Miley pulled down a granola bar and bag of chips. Though it wasn't the healthiest of meals, she was hungry and did not quite care. Four cupboards later, Miley had discovered the bowls and the cups.

She pulled down what she needed and then dumped some contents of chips into her bowl. Looking into the small fridge, Miley found a bottle of juice, which would suit her fancy and put the cup back away.

With everything she wanted in her hands she wound her way around the kitchen and into the small living room. She could hear the two men fighting outside the door but was too afraid to go back out there and ask why. After she finished her granola bar it had become silent.

She slowly ate her chips, listening for the existence of anyone outside. It had been nearly an hour when she could no longer hear either of the men outside. Knowing if she was going to have a chance to escape it would only be a small one… Miley quickly ran off to the kitchen grabbed another drink and raced to the door.

Yanking it open she was surprised when she did not find a man standing before it. Her feet could not move quickly enough as she shut the door behind her and raced to the edge of the deck.

"What do you think you are doing?" The voice of one of the men asked.

Miley froze. Whipping around to the sound, she smiled innocently at the man. "Uh…" She paused. "I was just bringing you a drink… thought you might be thirsty…" She said cautiously.

The man had stood and was now only a mere feet from her. His head was cocked slightly to the right listening to her.

"Oh, well thank you." He said surprised.

"You're welcome." Miley smiled. "You are… Nick or …" She began but he quickly interrupted.

"Nick." He said.

"Oh well, here you go Nick," she said sweetly holding the unopened bottle of juice up to him.

"Thanks." He said accepting the bottle.

"Do you mind if I sit with you…" Miley paused "it's boring inside… alone."

Nick looked around anxiously, and then shrugged his shoulders, "Sure."

Miley smiled and walked over to the swing which Nick had occupied. She curled herself up and turned to stare at him. What was it about these men that was so different than other men?

"So…" Miley said cautiously.

"Why are you here?" Nick asked cutting to the chase.

Miley looked away, she was considering not talking to this man. He was one of the guards that had brought her after all and he was a big and burly scary man… but she was scared. She wanted to go home, well that was a lie. She did not want to go home, this place was too beautiful.

"Work" was all she said. It was a slight whisper and Nick wasn't even sure she had said anything.

"Hmmm." He replied. "What do you do?" He continued.

Miley clamped her mouth shut and looked around at the scenery. What had she done wrong in her life to be held prisoner for doing who knew what?

"What did I do?" She finally snapped back at him.

Taken aback Nick sucked in a breath. He was about to speak when Cain walked back up. "Well…" Cain smirked. "What do we have here?"

"Uh Cain…" Nick muttered. "It's not like it looks."

Cain chuckled; he knew the guard was trying to get answers even if he was using the charm that he really did not possess. "Sure you were. Now," Cain said stepping up to the deck. "Miley, you need to get back inside. Dinner will be here shortly and we don't want anyone to have a conniption about you being out and about…" Cain said gently holding out a hand to her.

Miley nodded and silently stood up on her own. She did not accept the man's hand, instead she shyly ducked her head and continued inside.

Chapter 22

Sure enough, dinner did come shortly later. It was a yummy dinner of fish and rice, which Miley could get use to. Cain had carried it inside and set it on the small table.

Max and Derek arrived with Miley's luggage and placed everything that she did not need in a storage room, such as her tent and sleeping bag. She thanked them both for the care they had taken when packing her things.

Cain stood watch as Miley interacted with both the boys and as soon as they were gone he told her there was a bedroom in the back for when she decided she was tired and if she truly needed anything outside.

What she did not expect though when she went into the bedroom to change, was the gorgeous view. Miley really did not bother to move the curtains in the living room but she was sure it would have the same sight.

The bedroom was beautiful, but it made her nervous. Miley noticed just how truly open the home was. The room was completely open, sheer curtains swished in the breeze. The view was a lagoon and the only thing separating her from it was large glass French doors and windows finishing off one whole wall. An entire wall made out of glass. Miley was sure she had left behind the ocean but it was water none the less.

Miley's eyes explored the cream walls and beautiful paintings lining them. The floor was wood with beautiful exotic coloring to it and the bed… Well the bed hung suspended from thick woven ropes at the edge of the room overlooking the water.

Miley noticed a flowing waterfall at the far side and a sharp mountain cliff surrounding it. The cliff was covered in a soft green moss, which must have been from all the mist floating in the air.

Without looking around anymore, Miley turned around and began to strip her clothing. The spring dress, which she had been given, and now wearing was excessively cold for the night. It was about time she changed.

Piece by piece her clothing dropped to the floor. When she was standing there naked, looking for more clothing to put on a sound alerted her she was no longer alone. A rumbling purr flowed around her; Miley yelped and yanked the blanket from the bed, wrapping it around herself. "AH!" She screamed as she turned around and found two men ogling her suggestively raising their eyebrows at her on the other side of the glass window.

"Miley?" Max and Cain came bursting in. Nick had taken off to home, for the night and would return to guard her in the morning.

Miley whipped around as Max and Cain entered the room and screamed at them too. "What's …" Max began as he approached her slowly.

His eyes flit up and he noticed the two guards at the window grinning from ear to ear, turning his attention back down to Miley he noticed what was covering her. Smiling slightly he said "Are you naked?"

"Max!" Cain snapped.

"What?" Max asked turning his head back to Cain. "Look at those idiots and they are supposed to be guarding her not eye raping her."

Cain's head snapped over to the window and he growled. "Take her out of here," he hissed.

Since Miley was an unmated female, even though human, on the island it did not give any of the males a chance to peep for her arrival. Cain had trusted the two men out there to be good guards and make sure that Miley did not sneak out. NOT… ogle her as she changed and slept.

Cain stomped forward and through the sheer curtains onto the deck. "What do you think you are doing?" He hissed.

"Just watching as she changed. We weren't harming anyone," one of the men muttered.

"This …" Cain growled. "Is not acceptable. You two go to the front of the house. Guard the front door! Idiots," Cain hissed.

He turned around and stomped through the bedroom. After he had made his way out of the bedroom, he was even more shocked by the way, that Max was acting.

Miley whimpered as she held the blanket firmly around her body. Max purred in satisfaction, had pressed his arms against the wall beside Miley's head pinning her in place. His eyes were roaming her, he slowly lifted one hand and began to meander it beneath the blanket when Cain saw him. "Max!" he screamed snapping Max out of his mood.

Max's eyes snapped shut and he slowly opened them. Looking down slightly at Miley, he muttered his apologies. He had been in the right mind only moments before and was intent on being the guard, which he was but when he got her alone and something snapped inside him.

"Get out of here and go get Diesel," Cain snarled.

"What about you?" Max questioned.

"I'm a mated male. She's fine with me," Cain sighed. He turned his gaze to Miley and frowned. "I'm sorry. It's been a while since we had such a beautiful woman who is ah…" he paused, could he say mated and have her not question him… "Available," he decided.

"How do you know I'm available…?" She questioned with a pointed glare.

"Well…"

Cain did not know what else to say so he just wandered around the room for a moment, waiting for Diesel to show. Not long after Max had left he returned with Diesel at his side fuming angrily.

"What is going on out here?" He huffed as he stepped into the cabin. Miley's nakedness beneath the blanket took him off guard and he stiffed, purring in satisfaction before Cain cleared his throat disapprovingly.

"We have a problem."

Chapter 23

The problem was not the easiest to solve. Diesel quickly became protectively involved, in the situation and was acting strangely. "Miley let's go get you some clothes," Diesel said through grit teeth with flared nostrils.

He did not want her to get dressed, but he was having a hard time thinking clearly watching her fidget beneath that dang blanket.

Miley eyed the man for a moment then nodded. She turned to walk back into the bedroom, but stopped when she heard someone protesting behind her. "Diesel…" Cain complained.

Miley gazed between the two men and watched their interactions as Diesel just raised an eyebrow and snorted. He took a step around Cain and continued up to Miley, "Let's go," he said softly pressing a hand to her backside.

"I can change on my own…" Miley said quietly.

"And I have no guards on the deck…" Diesel replied.

"I really don't…" Miley began, but Diesel smirked quickly pushing her sideways into the wall and hovering above her.

"Right now… every one of the males on this island are going crazy and are tempted by you being here. Unless you want an incident where one of them loses control and ravishes that sexy little body of yours… including me… I would suggest you gather your clothing and change." Miley moaned slightly.

The man was so close he invoked tingles along her body. It was the kind of tingles that flowed through her until they knotted up in her stomach and urged her to reach out and touch him. However, Miley knew that would be a bad idea.

Growling at the sweet scent that was flowing from her, Diesel used all his might to push off from the wall. "Bathroom's over there."

Miley was frozen in place. She wanted for some reason, to touch this man, and it did not help that he hadn't worn a shirt and was hovering above her only moments ago.

"Go," he urged causing Miley to yelp and scurry to her luggage.

Miley slid into the bathroom quickly and dropped herself to the floor breathing hard. "What am I thinking? I am a prisoner here…" she whimpered. For some reason, that thought did not settle quite right and she desperately wanted to do something but what was that something… touch the man? No that would not be good enough, maybe … "Nope, bad thoughts!" Miley groaned.

After she had made it from changing in the bathroom, Diesel had told Max and Cain to guard from the porch.

"I'll deal with you in the morning," he grunted to Max. "I'm going to stay in here."

Miley quickly snapped her head toward Diesel worriedly. No… no… no he wasn't going to sleep with her… she wasn't up for that… or was she? It was so tempting but she would not tell him that.

"Diesel…" Cain complained.

"Cain…" Diesel retorted with a grunt. "Do as I command."

Cain sucked in a breath and grunted. "Miley, if you need either of us…" Cain said slowly.

"She won't," Diesel hissed.

Max gripped Cain's arm and tugged him out onto the deck.

"Go to sleep. I'll be on the chair," Diesel groaned.

"You're sleeping on the chair?" She questioned curiously. The man was big and the only chairs, which were in the room, were wicker chairs just large enough for her to be comfortable.

"Unless you are interested…" Diesel raised an eyebrow but stood firmly in place at the far side of the room.

"I can't let you sleep in the chairs…" Miley frowned. "It's not right for you."

"You are a prisoner here… and you are worried about me?" She could easily see the curiosity in his voice and the almost hopeful look to his eyes. The wonder of why a woman would give a crap if he was comfortable or not, was definitely in his mind.

"Why don't you sleep on the bed?" Miley said slowly pulling the covers back.

Diesel grinned and slowly walked forward, until Miley spoke again. "I'll sleep on the chair," she told him as she pushed herself from the bed.

Diesel let out a low chuckle and shook his head slowly. "Either we both sleep on the bed or I take the chair," he told her.

"I can't do that…" Miley said slowly. She could not sleep with this man and it could turn into something that she was not sure she was ready for. She did not know anything about him… yet she was on a remote island filled with hunky sexy men, one in particular which was in her bedroom right now… and she hadn't done something like this… But he looked so damn tempting!

"Okay…" Miley said slowly, mentally slapping herself as Diesel lurched forward grinning like a fool.

"Come on… time to sleep." He told her as he dropped into the bed.

Miley had fallen asleep quickly after her head hit the pillow of the strange dangling bed. The man beside her had curled his large body into the blankets and pulled them up over her gently. Beneath the blankets, she would have thought he would touch her, but not like this… She figured he would try and get her to jump his bones… but instead he slowly wound his arm around her waist and tugged her back into his chest, cuddling her. It wasn't long until they both had fallen into a peaceful slumber.

Chapter 24

When Miley had woke, the sun was up and shining brightly. A light wind flowed through the curtains of the room and Miley sucked in the scent of the warm tropical breeze.

She felt refreshed. It had been almost two weeks now since she had come to the island. Every day in the village, she wandered around the cabin feeling overly bored. She had been given her luggage and therefore she had found something in it to do… but she wanted out of the cabin.

Each day when she awoke, Diesel would be gone and would again arrive when she grew tired. He never did touch her in any way she was not quite comfortable with and she rather enjoyed the cuddling.

It was her seventh night here, during the middle of their slumber, when a young guard in training dared step inside the room and growl.

That was an interesting sight. Diesel was up and out of bed before she could barely register his movements. His fist shot out and he gripped the man by the throat thrusting him up against a wall. "Don't you dare growl at me, fledgling!" He hissed. His words slid off his tongue like a snake would probably sound if it could talk, full of hisses and 's's.

Miley scratched at her eyes trying to adjust to the sight before her. As soon as she got her bearings she was up and running across the room. "Diesel, what are you doing?!" She practically screamed as she yanked at his bulging muscular arms trying to free the boy.

Diesel slowly turned his head and eyed the human before him. She was cute in a vulnerable ignorant way. "Go back to bed." He said slowly.

"Let the boy go," she demanded.

No, he was not about to obey her, but the dominant tone in her voice was a turn on to him, and he liked it. Smirking slightly, Diesel grunted as he pushed the boy hard against the wall once again then let him drop to the floor. "Get out." He snapped.

"What the heck is wrong with you?" She questioned as she scrambled forward.

Diesel caught her in his arms before she could get to the boy and pulled her close. "He'll be fine, he shouldn't have intruded." He purred.

It had not taken more than a few seconds for the boy to come to his senses and scramble out of the room.

Diesel directed Miley back to the bed and held her in his arms while he curled down into the bed. "I like you." He purred into her ear. He was so close it sent shivers down her spine.

Miley frowned. She liked him too, but it was not like anything between them would happen, she was his prisoner and he had to protect her from ever man on the island. Instead of saying, what she really wanted to Miley snorted, "It's strange how a prisoner can invite such an emotion in you."

"Ha." Diesel chuckled. "If you would tell me the answer to my questions then you probably wouldn't be considered a threat any longer, but you know you will never go back home…" He reminded her.

"If I answered your questions you'd be done with me and probably kill me!" She grunted. Miley knew that would not happen but she felt the urge to push the envelope.

"Right, well if you want to be treated like a prisoner then I'll treat you like a prisoner...," he growled then something in him changed. It was like Diesel was struggling with an inner voice and he smirked, "better yet..."

That unnerved her and Miley struggled to push away from him. Instead of getting far, Diesel's grip tightened on her and he rolled her over and perched himself over top of her.

Miley's eyes widened but she was not afraid. She was excited. Diesel had never shown much dominance laced with interest in her before and the lust was wafting off him in waves. His violet eyes sparked, shimmering through the darkness, "What are you going to do bad boy?" she teased. As soon as the words left her mouth, Miley slapped her hand over top her lips and stared up at Diesel wide eyed. She could not believe she had just said that.

Diesel smirked. "You are so beautiful. So..." he dragged out as he leaned down and began to suckle her sensitive skin "tempting." He purred.

Miley shuttered and gulped. For some reason she knew this day would come. The tension between them had been growing and she desperately wanted it to develop.

Something once again snapped inside the man and Diesel grunted as he pushed himself up and away from Miley almost as if he had flown backward. "We will talk in the morning." He said quickly yanking on his jeans. Diesel had elected to sleep in his boxers after the second day when he must have figured Miley was comfortable enough with him around.

"Cain and Derek are outside if you need anything." He almost whispered.

Miley could not quite grasp what had just happened. She had practically invited him to have sex with her and he just took off. Was there something wrong with her?

Chapter 25

Miley had been wallowing so much in her own self-pity since Diesel had practically stormed out; that she barely slept a wink. When the sun finally began to rise, Miley pulled herself from bed. She did not feel like getting dressed. She did not feel like taking a shower, which she happily learned about days ago. Instead, she slowly dragged herself into the living room and curled up in a blanket sulking.

Miley puffed out a breath. She could not stand it sitting around here any longer. She was going to go and find something to do. She could not believe Diesel left her frustrated. She was lonely, bored, and hot. She stood up and stomped back to the bedroom. She wanted to change into something that would attract everyone's eye.

Quickly, she focused all her attention on the dresser she had loaded her clothing into. Though she hadn't really brought anything absolutely drop dead sexy, Miley did bring her new swimsuits and though the men who had brought her here and Diesel himself have seen one of them but her secret weapon was a bright blue string bikini that really brought out her eyes.

Knowing better than to change in the bedroom with who knows who out there watching… Miley grabbed the swimsuit and walked down the hall to the bathroom.

With her swimsuit on and her hair pulled up into a messy bun, Miley continued out to the deck outside the bedroom. Slowly, she peeked her head out the window, looking for guards.

Fortunately, there was no guard in sight. Diesel had ordered the guards away from the bedroom. With no one in sight, she looked out toward the water and smiled. The scorching heat of the island would be smothered out quickly with the cool water. Miley patted her way across the decking until she came to the edge and looked down searching for hidden rocks or shoreline.

A grin adorned Miley's lips as she backed away for the edge before quickly running toward it again. As she hit the edge Miley jumped. "Wahoo!" She screamed out. A breath of fresh air surged around her as she landed in the cool water.

Miley felt anew. The water was refreshing and the air outside was invigorating. She swam across the lagoon and then back, enjoying her 'forbidden' free time.

As Miley rose from the water for the umpteenth time a voice called out to her. "Well you're not the usual sacrifice." Someone mumbled and Miley quickly snapped her head toward the sound. She was now staring wide-eyed at the figure of a man as she floated within the lagoon. He was tall with tanned skin from spending so much time in the sun similar to Diesel. His chest was bare, sculpted, with a beautifully colored dragon tattoo encased his body across his taught abs to his well defined shoulders and even laced around his 'could squish me to death' muscular arms. To say this man was beautiful would be an understatement.

"Huh?" Miley asked dumbly blinking up at him.

"So who's the lucky man? I was unaware that there was a sacrifice." The man said scratching his chin, he had been gone for a while but he wasn't expecting a new sacrifice in the area.

"What are you talking about?" Miley said swimming away from him.

Orion hadn't expected the woman to act so strangely. Most of the sacrifices did not act like this. Most of them were shy and nervous for a while before they accepted their mate and this girl certainly hadn't accepted her mate.

"Who's your mate?" Orion asked knowing he should congratulate the man.

"Mate?" Miley frowned. She could not figure out what he was talking about. Instead of paying any more attention, she swam away from the man toward the waterfall. She was going to enjoy herself out here.

Orion wasn't thrilled with the blatant disobedience and the woman ignoring him. He would have her talk to him one way or another. She would obey his word like every other clan member below him. Orion had not planned on a swim, he was, yet to speak with his alpha when he had arrived back home and spotted a new woman. Annoyed, he rushed forward taking himself into the water. By the time the girl had risen from the water, he was there.

"I do not accept people ignoring my questions." Orion growled out, he was beta for a reason.

"Oh!" Miley squeaked pressing her hand to her breast. "You scared me."

Orion reached forward and grabbed hold of the girl's wrist pulling her into him firmly. Shocks of electricity shimmied up between them, "What is your name?" He asked changing subject.

Miley sniffed the air between them sighing, leaning forward before she snapped back to reality. "I don't know what you're talking about! I'm not giving you my name." Miley scowled trying to pull away. The men here were strange and dominating, which bothered her.

"Orion!" Diesel called out as he rushed toward the edge of the lagoon. He knew this would eventually be a problem. He would have told him about the girl but he had been away. "Miley, this is my second in command, Orion."

Orion smiled with pride. "Now…" Orion had begun as he once again tugged Miley forward. "Who is your mate?"

Flash of anger adorned Diesel's enthralling eyes before quickly diminishing. "Leave her, Orion."

"I need a mate." Orion said huskily as he leaned closer to Miley.

"She's mine." Diesel breathed and Orion released his hold quickly dropping Miley's wrist and moving away slightly as he clenched his fists tightly.

"It's an honor to have someone so…" He paused and leaned back as if he was evaluating her "tempting around here." He murmured sucking in a breath. Orion turned and swam away diving beneath the water and disappearing.

Miley looked over to Diesel, her attention now fully on his beautiful being, and let out a breath. Diesel rolled his eyes "Get out of the water Miley."

"I'm rather enjoying my time here." Miley muttered. It was a very familiar situation and she knew he could easily drag her out of the water.

"Don't push it." Diesel groaned.

"Push what?" Miley pressed.

"My control," Diesel replied huskily. "Now get out of the water and go inside. We'll talk later." With that, Diesel turned to walk away.

"Hey?" Miley grunted as she swam toward the edge of the water. Diesel's allusiveness was annoying her. She wanted that talk and she wanted it now. She did not feel like a prisoner other than the staying in the guesthouse thing. She felt more like a lover that just was not getting any love.

This man, Diesel, the man who had been staying with her in her guest room, did not give her the stay-a-way vibe like Victor had. She remembered the strange man that had dropped her here and knew she needed to talk to Diesel about him. If anything, Miley felt she should pull herself closer and suck in Diesel's delicious scent. Huh? Miley sniffed the air and sighed.

In a foggy haze, Miley swam over to the edge of the lagoon. It was as if the men here had a hold on her and she could not quite see through the fog. Now with Diesel and Orion's disappearance, Miley could think better.

"Strange." Miley groaned. When she was far enough in she could stand, Miley stood and continued her way back up to the deck outside the bedroom.

The swim was fun while it had lasted until the two men had ruined it. She was muttering and complaining to herself as she grabbed angrily at fresh pieces of clothing then stomped down the hallway to the bathroom to change.

When she finished dressing, Miley brushed her hair a bit then continued to the door. She was going to go find Diesel. She wanted his speech and she had one of her own to give him.

Chapter 26

Miley was surprised and yet not at all surprised when she opened the front door to two men sitting on the porch. "Where do you think you're going?" Cain questioned.

For a moment, Miley paused in her steps and hesitated in her thoughts. Was she guarded because she was a prisoner or because of the strange attacks?

She figured she would at least try. "I am going to see Diesel," she said semi-confidently.

Cain nodded his head slowly. Miley was sure he was going to refuse her. "Okay, I'll bring you to him. He said it was okay when you decided to come and visit him." What? Why hadn't she thought of that earlier?

Cain stood "Well, are you coming?" He asked.

"Yep," Miley said quickly hurrying forward."

As they walked toward the house, Miley felt as if she needed to fill the silence with conversation but was too nervous. Instead, she walked along side Cain in silence.

"Right this way." Cain said softly holding out his arm for Miley to precede him.

Miley stepped inside the large home, took in the fresh smell of baked goods, and moaned slightly. "Lunch is being prepared," Cain smiled.

"It smells good." Miley commented.

"Sure does." He replied with a smile. "Here we are." Cain said holding up his hand to knock on the door.

With a few swift knocks of his fist, Cain smiled down at Miley reassuringly. "He's going to be happy to see you."

Miley wasn't so sure about that. She knew he wouldn't be happy. He would probably scold her for bothering him, yet he said they had to talk and she desperately wanted to know what he was thinking about.

"What is it?" Diesel hissed out and Miley flinched slightly. Though it wasn't quite the flinch she thought she would have, it was more of a shiver of excitement that was beginning to build inside her.

"It's Cain. May I come in?" Cain called out.

"Proceed." Diesel huffed.

When Cain smiled down at Miley once again and reached forward to open the door, Miley sucked in a breath. "Wait," she whispered.

"No, it's alright." Cain chuckled.

"What if he …" she begun, but never got to finish.

"Miley?" Diesel's voice was happier than a moment ago. "What brings you?"

Miley smiled softly. "You said we could talk."

Diesel's head turned slightly and Miley then realized he wasn't alone. Sitting were Miley could not quite see at first was the man from the water, Orion. "Of course. Ri, could you give us a few minutes?" Diesel asked.

Orion nodded and stood up walking toward Miley before pausing for a sniff. "Mesmerizing," he murmured.

Miley sucked in a nervous breath and backed up slightly. A growl from the far side of the room made her lose her nervousness, turn her head away from the man, and settle her attention on Diesel. His shoulders were tensing along with his body. "Get out." He said through gritted teeth.

Miley slowly backed up and Cain chuckled. "He's not talking to you dear." He pushed gently on her back "Go on. I'll be out here when you're finished."

Miley stumbled forward and quickly turned her head to catch sight of Cain and Orion disappearing behind the door. "Come here" Diesel said huskily. "I won't hurt you."

"I don't know…" Miley muttered. "Right now you're kind of scaring me."

Diesel's eyes flicked shut and he sucked in a breath, slowly releasing it through his nostrils. "I don't like anyone taking what's mine." He huffed.

Miley did not quite understand that. She frowned and looked at him with furrowed brows, "What's yours?"

"Sit down?" He asked.

"Answer me." Miley groaned.

Diesel snorted. "Let's go for a walk." He said after an exaggerated pause and pushed his chair back to stand.

"Why?" Miley groaned.

"We need to talk so we'll walk and talk, more relaxing outside. Easier to talk," he said with a tight smile.

Diesel reached Miley's side and wrapped an arm around her waist. "Do you mind?" He questioned.

"Uh…" Miley sputtered "no."

"Great." He grinned.

The two then began to walk out of the office and out of the house into the island breeze.

Chapter 27

The sun was high in the air and it warmed the island. "What's yours?" Miley asked anxiously.

"There are things about this island that you just don't know…" Diesel dragged out.

"Like what?" Miley questioned.

"You'll find out in time." Diesel sighed. Switching topics, he looked at her with a small grin. "I like you." He breathed out.

Diesel may have been a great leader and a grown man but he had never said those words to a woman before. He had never liked any of the woman whom were sacrificed before and he never really had known any of the local main-land-er woman either.

It had been a long time since Diesel even felt the love that he felt for Miley. Yes, he has not known her for long but she dug right into his heart and made a nest there.

Yes, she wasn't like him, but there wasn't any woman that could be like him. This woman was different though. Something about her that he felt connected too. Something that made him want her all to himself.

Yes, there was once mates… but that also died along with the lack of female dragon births years ago. Miley had stopped in her tracks and was staring at him. The man was lost in thought. "Are you alright?" she asked.

He snapped out of his thoughts and turned to her, with an enormous grin on his face he purred. The look made Miley's nerves go all over. She slowly backed away from him, which caused Diesel to growl. "I want you." He growled inhumanly.

"Diesel you're scaring me right now." Miley cringed slightly backing away.

Diesel took in the steps that Miley took and he continued toward her with larger ones. As Miley's back bumped into something hard she yelped and anxiously felt behind her. A tree. Crap.

"I always get what I want," Diesel said in his beautiful accent and Miley could not help but feel as if she was going to melt inside.

Before she could say anything Diesel entrapped Miley with his arms and the tree behind her. "Kiss me." He told her.

"Diesel," Miley mumbled.

Noticing her reluctance, Diesel seized the moment, leaning in quickly and capturing her lips in his own.

Diesel purred as his lips moved along Miley's. It took a moment but she did respond happily, melting into his chest and kissing him back.

When Diesel finally pulled away, Miley sucked in a breath. One hand went up to press against her tender kiss swollen lips and the other reached out and slapped him hard across the face.

Chapter 28

Tears streamed down Miley's face. She had felt taken advantage of and it unsettled her. There was never a man who she had been even remotely liked this much and now she wasn't sure what to do with herself.

Had he taken advantage of the opportunity and kissed her? Or was she desperate for that kiss as much as he was? She was so conflicted.

As Miley ran through the small village, alarms sounded above her. They were terrifyingly loud, almost like a tornado siren, and it hurt her ears. Her hands slapped over her ears and she tried to block out the noise.

"Miley!" Diesel yelled. He had stood there stunned, but as soon as the sirens began, he knew he needed to get to her and protect her.

"Diesel?" She called back, knowing that he could not hear her.

He caught up with her in no time. Wrapping an arm around Miley's tiny waist, he pulled her into his chest. "We got to go!" He yelled into her ear.

The noise was deafening and blocking out most of what she heard, but Miley did not protest as Diesel led her away.

"What's going on?" she cried out.

"Intruders!" he shouted back.

"What?" Miley questioned. She figured she must have heard the wrong thing.

"Alpha!" someone shouted and Diesel turned quickly to face the owner of the voice.

Miley screeched and Diesel sighed, tugging her tighter. "It's okay." he murmured. "Jonah, what's going on?"

A tall beast stood before them, his wings erect, and his body semi ridged. He bowed down slightly and lowered his head as he began to speak. "An intruder has been spotted on the north beach. He says he's looking for someone but we know he's from the Dugan Clan. We can smell it."

"Have him detained. I will be there shortly to help with questioning. Thank you Jonah" Diesel nodded his head respectfully, "you're dismissed."

The mammoth beast scrunched down and before Miley could even take a breath it was up in the air and gone. She was left stunned and afraid. Did she really just see what she thought she had saw?

Diesel was walking with her tucked into his side. She had run toward a place she had not quite seen before and he was now leading her toward it. Beneath their feet formed a small foot trail beaten path worn away over the years by continuous use.

Ahead of them lie the ocean but before that was a spectacular sight. Massive stone structures of near replicas to the giant, which had flown away before Miley's very eyes. "What is this place?" Miley stuttered out.

Diesel stopped and dropped his grip on her as he slowly walked toward the statue and turned around sharply on his heels. "Don't lie to me…" Diesel grit out through tightly clenched teeth, "Is the intruder searching for you?"

Chapter 29

Miley sucked in a breath and stared at the man before her. Diesel was intimidating, his back straight and his shoulders broad, he towered over her easily. She looked down and shook her head slightly.

"I would assume." Miley sighed.

Diesel growled. He was trying to find the words to say but it was just so hard to do. "Are you part of the Dugan Clan!" he nearly yelled.

Miley cringed at his tone and looked up abruptly, "what are you talking about?" She questioned.

"I know you're not mated and I know you're human, but are you …," Diesel groaned. He sure hoped she wasn't going to be joined to someone, he liked her and for some reason she settled his dragon. "Are you betrothed to someone from the Dugan?"

This time Miley laughed "What? Getting married, you have to be kidding."

Diesel growled again this time rushing toward her, his arms reached out and he gripped her waist as he brought her back against the rocks of a nearby statue. He pinned her there. "What are these people looking for you?" he growled out.

"Diesel…" Miley said calmly. "You have kept me locked up in your beautiful village for how long now?" She paused trying to figure out the time frame. "The man who dropped me here was sure to come looking for me eventually," she shrugged.

Diesel's expression changed from straight up pissed off to confused and curious. "Who brought you here, Miley."

Miley let out a breath and gently pushed at Diesel's chest, freeing up some breathing space. "Can we sit?" She asked quietly.

Diesel nodded his head and followed Miley over to the lower rocks for a place to sit. "I was asked to document the island, photograph creatures, and take notes on what this island has to hidden here. I am a photographer; a magazine company called me and paid for the trip. Victor," Miley was interrupted by a deep rumbling growl in Diesel's chest and she shuttered as she looked up into his eyes, there were the most brilliant shade of purple she had ever saw, scary and not human.

"That bastard!" Diesel roared.

"I know he left me here," Miley sneered.

"You have no idea…" Diesel groaned.

"What was that creature?" Miley questioned, quickly changing the subject.

"A dragon," Diesel replied nonchalantly.

Her vision blurred and Miley wavered slightly. She was sure it had been a dream, a hallucination caused by the deafening noise she had heard earlier.

"Just like those from the Dugan," Diesel continued.

Miley could not see him. Her vision had turned to a quickly narrowing tunnel and before she could fully hear his next sentence, everything went black.

Chapter 30

"Well, that was a very human reaction." Diesel said as he rubbed a cool washcloth against Miley's forehead.

"Diesel?" Miley mumbled.

"Yeah, I'm right here. I take it you have never seen anyone shift in the Dugan Clan?" he asked.

"I don't have a clue what you're talking about," Miley groaned as she reached up to rub her face.

"I have to go and interview our prisoner; Cain make sure she's steady before she stands up," Diesel demanded. "Keep an eye on here, I'll be back later."

Miley blinked and turned her head slightly watching Diesel's muscled retreating back as he walked away. She wished desperately she could run her fingers across the taught muscles there. However, she had mixed feelings. What if he turned out to be a cheater, just like Toby?

"You know drool isn't very attractive…" Cain laughed.

"What?" Miley replied flabbergasted.

"He likes you too but right now he's confused as to why you're here. It would help everything if you would just tell us why you're here, Miley," Cain said taking the towel from Miley and handing her a cup of water.

"I told him," Miley scolded, she was confused.

"Nobody knows about this island and those that do are afraid to come here." Cain scoffed. "We know you're lying about something."

"I am not lying. I was abandoned here after I was promised a big raise and really good royalties on my photos. I should be home now and wallowing in my newly found riches!" Miley hissed. It was practically true at least. She would be at home and wallowing but not in riches… more like sorrow and heartache.

"You know, you humans are all the same!" Cain snapped. "I don't understand how you all could be so money hungry!"

"Money hungry!" Miley snapped. "What would I possibly be looking for here money wise? This island is so secluded I doubt any of you make a living."

Cain had been nice enough before, but now he was just pissing her off. There was no money here to be hungry for. "Wait… humans?" Miley questioned once she registered what Cain had said. "You are human!"

A deep laughter erupted within Cain and he turned sharply to walk toward the door. "If I was human, I wouldn't be living here." He told her as he slowly disappeared.

That made Miley question everything. Everything Diesel had said earlier, the 'dragon', now even Cain, all of it was confusing; everything she had known about the world was crashing down around her.

Chapter 31

Miley stretched and sat up to look around. Cain had left her in a bedroom but she had doubt he had gone far. Surveying the room, she took in account the very different décor from the décor in the guesthouse. This looked more like the main house, which Diesel lived in.

The walls were a bright white with teal drapes and a teal cover on the bed. Unfolding herself from the sheets, she realized that the room was rather cool and the drapery swayed in the wind. Someone had left the window open and that made her curious.

Miley pushed herself up from the bed, steadying herself before moving against the bed frame, then wobbled slightly toward the breezy window. It was a beautiful sunset. The tree line glowed from the sun's rays, it was getting dark.

She was on the second floor of the house; it must have been the main home, Diesel's home. As her feet hit the still warm wood of the deck, someone stepped out from nowhere.

"Well, I guess I can see why the alpha has kept you locked up. Victor did not tell me you were so beautiful." The man's voice was gravely and he held such a tone that just screamed 'Do not trust me!'

"Who are you?" Miley said cautiously.

"I am alpha of the Dugan Clan, my dear. I am going to take you away from here. Poor Jamie has caused such an uproar and Alpha McBride seems to be very busy right now." The man chuckled.

Miley eyed him. He made her nervous. The man had graying hair that was once some dark color, his eyes were grey green and he looked very untrustworthy. He took a step closer, reaching out a hand and Miley hesitantly took a step back.

"How do you know Victor?" Miley said.

"Ah I see you remember him." The man replied.

"That bastard abandoned me here!" Miley snapped.

"I know, I know and I'm sorry for that. I thought that was in the email that you would be staying here by yourself, better working environment you know." The man shrugged. "Anyway if you would please…"

Miley stepped back again but it wasn't quite far enough because before her very eyes the man began to change. His skin rippled and his head tipped back as he spoke words that she could not quite understand but one phrase she recognized from the English language was "Take me!" right before his whole body covered in scales and expanded into a massive creature.

Miley screamed but it was too late. The massive dragon hopped down from a perch on the deck railing and roared as he knocked her down to the ground, his claws pinning her and its large fangs dripping with saliva as he roared.

"This will be over soon and you'll be home in your apartment." The dragon said, , it shouldn't be able to talk, and like everything else it confused her. A bubbly mist spewed out of the beast's mouth and soon Miley was passing out as the beast wrapped his talons around her waist and lofted them into the air with his massive wings.

Chapter 32

"NO!" Max yelled as he rushed into the room and witnessed a massive grey brown dragonfly up into the air. There was no way for him to catch the beast; he had not acquired the quick speed shifting yet. He stood helpless hoping his brother did not maim him when he heard the news.

Cain had left him in charge of one of the most important task possible in this clan, protecting and keeping an eye on the alpha's future mate. Now he screwed up by not being in the room watching her while Cain did whatever Cain was doing.

Max had rushed back through the house and down to the security locked door of the dungeon. "I need to see Diesel right away!" Max huffed, he was breathing hard and panted as he stared down a fellow clan member.

"My duty is to guard this door. Nobody goes in or out without the alpha's or beta's permission, and you do not have permission." The guard told him.

"Either you move," Max warned, "or the fact that the girl that the alpha is in love with is missing, will be on your head." The last of Max's words were a near hiss and the guard's eyes went wide while he quickly moved out of the way.

"Thank you." Max rolled his eyes.

"Diesel!" Max yelled as soon as he was on the other side of the door; he was running now. His words were panicked.

Max jumped down the staircase and his feet practically floated as he ran full tilt through the dungeon. "Alpha!" he yelled.

"Max?" Orion questioned. He was standing in front of a prisoner's cell. "What's wrong Max? Why are you down here, I'm going to have that guard's head!"

"Where's Diesel?" He hurried.

"He's up in his office. He had to do some searches…" Orion replied. "Why?"

Max growled. He whipped around and was running back toward the stairs before Orion could even question. Orion groaned and sprinted after the man. "Max, what's wrong" he demanded.

Max panted painfully. He wanted desperately to run toward his alpha but his beta was demanding and he could not refuse the order. With a grunt Max stopped. Taking a deep breath, Max said, "Miley's in danger."

"Go." Orion replied, signaling for he was free to go. With that though, Orion too left quickly. The prisoner was secured.

When both men made it to the entryway, Orion told the guard to keep watch of the prisoner then hurried away after Max.

Orion quickly led the way, being a beta he was faster and stronger than the smaller Max. He burst through the office door. Both men let out a frustrated growl when they were greeted with an empty room.

"Where is he?" Max snapped, though he really had no right to question the alpha's were abouts.

Orion was about to speak, he was about to say something on the lines of 'crap', when both men turned their attention to the devastated, disgruntled, and peeved roar. The two turned knowing they would be finding the alpha very soon.

Chapter 33

"What do you mean she's gone?" Diesel roared.

Fury was evident in his bright violet eyes. Max was staring at the floor not meeting Diesel's eyes. "I told Cain to watch her!" Diesel snarled. "Where is he?"

"The Dugan clan alpha stole her," Max said urgently. "I could not stop him."

"He what! Where was Cain?" Diesel was beyond angry. His body shook with fury and he was moments from shifting out of rage.

"Cain's missing right now." Orion shrugged. "We'll deal with him later. Right now we have to attack the Dugan Clan."

Diesel stomped the short distance to the door. As his feet hit the porch the beast within could not take it any longer. Diesel jumped forward shifting into his massive dragon without hesitation. A roar ripped from his lungs, calling to his clan, he was calling for war.

Chapter 34

Miley awoke feeling extremely well rested. Her body felt calm and she felt like she had slept for ages. Slowly she sat up and rubbed the sleep from her eyes. Everything felt dreamy. Looking around, Miley realized she was in her bedroom.

Trying hard to remember how she had gotten to her room, Miley simply could not place what had happened. Spotting her phone on the bedside table, she grabbed at it urgently. The last day she had remembered according to her cell was nearly a month ago. She frowned.

"Where was I?" she groaned.

The next thing Miley noticed was her email updates on the cell phone. One-hundred and six new emails; clicking on the oldest email she had, Miley read the subject line, "Your trip has been confirmed."

She had taken a trip, but to where. Continuing to read more of the subject lines soon she came to ones that read "have a fun trip" and then a few days later "where are you we're worried."

When Miley read the 'we're worried' subject lines in her emails, she became worried herself. She clicked on the email. It was from her sister, the very same sister, whom she is only on limited speaking terms with. Normally someone worrying about her being gone for too long wouldn't as quickly of worried her but the message from her sister being worried made Miley confused.

Miley's sister would have never worried about her unless she missed something important. Looking back a few emails, she also noticed many other people having the same type of urgent messages.

I'm worried, Miles where are you!

That one was from her friend.

Quickly Miley abandoned her emails grasping the phone and dialing Morgan.

"MILEY!" Morgan screamed into the phone and not even a breaths moment later there was pounding on Miley's apartment door.

Miley groaned and hung up the phone before padding her way across the apartment. "Take it easy," she hissed softly as she swung the door open to come face to face with a very excited and anxious Morgan.

"Where have you been?" Morgan complained.

"I don't…" Miley began and then looked around before saying anything else. It seemed strange being here and she was not quite sure why. "I don't really know…"

Morgan frowned looking at her friend. "How do you not know?" She huffed slamming her hands to her hips. "First you come to me and say you're going to some exotic island and not taking me and then you're gone for like ever. Nobody has so much as heard a word about where you have been. I stopped by your work and Charlie said he figured you quit without telling him and he found a replacement already!"

"What?" Miley sighed rubbing her temples. Why did her head hurt so much? "The last thing I remember…" Miley said and paused trying to remember what it was she remembered, "was I don't quite know…"

"Come on sweetie sit down. Maybe you hit your head or something." Morgan insisted. With her friend's arm in her hand, Morgan began to drag Miley over to the couch.

Miley sat down without much protest rubbing her head as she flopped backward. "I'll get you something to drink. Do you think I need to take you to the hospital?" Morgan said walking toward the kitchen.

Miley was about to speak when she heard Morgan yell from the kitchen "What the heck is this?"

Miley sighed as she pushed herself up and wandered into the kitchen. There it was; the object of Morgan's obvious confusion, a note clearly not in Miley's handwriting.

Miley,

Don't forget your article and photos taken at the island. We are eagerly awaiting your contributions. Check your camera.

Victor.

"Who's Victor?" Morgan asked curiously.

Miley's brows furrowed and her face crunched up as she tried to remember. "Honestly," she said looking over at Morgan, "I don't really remember. Where's my camera?" She finished looking around and quickly spotting it on the kitchen table.

As Miley quickly flicked on the camera and passed from picture to picture her eyes began to bulge. Everything now was all now becoming clear but she just knew she could not tell her friend.

She could not tell anyone and those pictures… she could not put those up for the world to see.

She groaned and slumped her shoulders as she stumbled backward catching herself on the counter top. "Miley, are you okay? You look a little pail." Came Morgan's response but Miley just grumbled, clutched the camera to her chest and ran to her bedroom.

Chapter 35

"What the heck?" Morgan complained as she raced after Miley. Miley had slammed the bedroom door and locked it before Morgan could reach it and slammed her back against it. She could not let Morgan see those pictures.

"It's okay. I've…" Miley struggled for the words to say, "I've got to go to the bathroom a minute. I'll be right out."

"You know how hard it was to track you down?" a man's voice boomed and Miley gasped in surprise as she turned her head to face him.

"Who are you?" She questioned with a scrunched up face. He looked familiar but she just could not place him.

"You don't remember me?" The man frowned. "That's unfortunate."

"I'm sorry but I'm having a hard time placing your face," she shrugged. "Can you remind me?" Miley said slowly standing up.

For some reason, the man felt trust worthy. She knew deep down she trusted him, even if she could not remember him. It was as if she had known him for years.

"I guess, it's normal to forget when you've been gone for so long and I'm sure he used amnesia potion on you." The man said slowly stepping forward.

She thought about that. Where had she been and for how long? Miley pressed herself backward and to the side. Though she felt as if she trusted the man with all her heart, she still could not remember him and it was making her nervous.

"Don't do that." The man complained as he stepped closer to her once again.

"Do what?" Miley replied quietly, taking another step away.

"That," The man groaned. "Don't move away from me."

"I don't know you," Miley said defensively.

"You do, you just have to remember." He shrugged and with two large steps, he surrounded her with his arms, pinning her to the wall.

"Leave me alone," She said in a squeak.

"I can't do that." He rolled his eyes.

A sharp knock on the door made Miley turn her head toward it. "I'll be right there," Miley would have said to Morgan, but the man spoke up first.

"Darling, Miley's busy right now, I'll have her call you later."

Miley's eyes bulged and she turned toward the man with a sharp glare. How dare he speak up and tell her friend she was with him?

"Miley, are you alright," Morgan asked.

"Tell her to leave." The man said in a soft tone.

Without another thought, the words left Miley's mouth, "I think you should go home. I'll call you later."

A choked giggle and cough mixture burst from Morgan's lips and Miley was sure she was covering her mouth as she spoke,

"I'm soooo sorry about interrupting Miles. I'll come back later. Don't forget, I want details."

With that, Miley could hear Morgan's footfalls as she walked across the apartment and out the door.

"How did you get in here?" she questioned.

"My dear, there is so much you don't know about our kind." The man said in a thick accented voice announced as he strode toward her.

She cried, "Stay away from me!"

"I can't do that," he frowned.

"I'll call the cops!" Miley threatened, though it felt so wrong. Something made her feel like she needed to be close to him.

"Lovely... I would be gone before they got here and back as soon as they were gone. They cannot catch me." He purred. The man was so close now but Miley could not find it in herself to run and hide in the closet or even the bathroom. Nope... she stood frozen.

"Get away," she stuttered out.

"As much as I would love to give you everything you want...," the man said slowly. In the blink of an eye, he was so close he grabbed her wrist yanking her into his chest. "It's taken a lot to find you, and your disappearance has caused my kind, to go into war."

"Huh?" Miley replied confused.

"Listen love, I would love to have you to myself, but my alpha wants you and that's how it's going to be. Why don't you pack your things…?" the man told her as he leaned down. His words lightly caressed her ear as he spoke.

"No?" Miley replied nervously. She wasn't quite sure she wanted a man in her life; she had yet to rid it of Toby completely.

"Don't make me guard you until he comes to get you… I really don't want to do that. The war is still going on and until I bring you back…" he said shaking his head slightly, "it will never be finished. Diesel is…"

"Diesel?" Miley said quickly interrupting the man. She remembered the name and it elicited feelings deep within her.

"Yeah," The man said slowly. "He's been searching for you, we took out the Dugan, but he can't accept both the Dugan and our clan fully and be the alpha he really should be without being fully mated."

"I can't leave. This is my home," Miley said quickly changing subjects.

The man groaned, quickly shoving his hand in his pocket and yanking out a cell phone. He dialed then spoke into it moments later. "Yeah, it's Orion, I found her."

The voice on the other side of the phone was muffled, but Miley still could recognize it slightly. "Yep, I'll keep an eye on her, track the number, and send him right away. I want to go home." Orion snorted.

"Sounds great; I'll see him then." Orion grinned and looked down at Miley. "Bye."

"Who's coming?" She questioned curiously.

The grin on Orion's face turned into a full-blown smile, "your mate."

Chapter 36

It took some encouraging but Orion let Miley walk away from him to use the bathroom, getting the breather she desperately needed.

After a little while of getting her breather, Miley returned to her room to find Orion gone. When she walked out of the bedroom, she found him scrounging in the fridge in the kitchen. "You have anything here too eat?" he asked lifting his head out the fridge and looking at her.

"No." Miley said slowly. "But I'm starving too." It had been late afternoon when she had awoken and now it was past dinnertime. Food had been pushed onto the back burner for a while.

"Are you ever going to leave?" Miley asked.

"Not till he gets here." Orion shrugged. "It was hard finding you."

"Fine," Miley grunted. She stomped from the room, being followed by Orion. "I'm going to get something to eat."

"Whoa, whoa, whoa…." Orion huffed out, rapidly making it across the room to block the apartment door. "Where do you think you're going?"

"If I am ever going to get something to eat… I have to go and get it. I haven't been home in a while." Miley reminded him.

"I'm not letting you go," Orion protested, "do you have any idea how hard it was to find you?"

"Grrr…" Miley huffed as she turned around, "No I have no idea, I've live here for a long time, I could easily find myself. Why would you have been looking for me so hard for anyway?"

"Can't you just order something, isn't that what city people do?" Orion groaned.

Miley sighed. She could definitely order in, but generally, she just went down to get what she wanted. "Fine," she said finally, "I'll call," she walked over into the kitchen and pulled out a menu. "This is the place I'm ordering from, what do you want?"

Orion mulled it over and when Miley returned from her room with her cell phone, he had chosen what looked good. She made the call and then went to the fridge for a drink.

The pair decided to sit down in the living room while they waited. Miley stared nervously ahead over her at the television that was not turned on; while Orion stared at Miley making sure she did not disappear before his eyes.

"Why are you staring at me?" Miley finally questioned him.

"I'm sorry, it's just that it was hard finding you and Diesel had men searching for you in many different areas of the city…" he dragged out.

"He had men all over looking for me?" Miley asked surprised.

"Don't look so surprised," Orion chuckled softly "Once a dragon finds a woman he wants for himself, they never let her go."

Miley's heart warmed at the thought of having a man who would never stray or betray her. "I don't remember him much…," she said slowly.

"You will soon. The effects will wear off by the time he gets here I'm sure." Orion said even if it was not entirely true, he hoped she would.

After an awkward dinner, Miley offered up some blankets and a pillow to Orion. "I would rather sleep in the same room as you," he told her.

"I don't think that's a good idea." Miley answered.

Orion smiled "It wasn't a request, it was more of an 'it's gonna happen type deal.' It's my head if something happens to you between now and when Diesel arrives."

Miley shifted anxiously from foot to foot and looked around the apartment, thinking of what to do. Then the idea popped into her head. Turning on her heals she sprinted through down the hall.

A chuckle erupted from Orion's chest, deep and full of humor. Before Miley could question, strong arms wrapped around her waist, pulled her to a stop, and spun her around, so she was pinned to the wall.

"Ah playful are we?" Orion questioned huskily into Miley's ear.

She gasped and looked down at her feet to afraid to meet the beautiful man's eyes. "I could play all day darling but you will tire eventually." He whispered.

"Please," Miley shuttered slightly as a plan formed in her mind, "I just want a moment…"

Orion pulled back from her, looking into her eyes and searching them. It was as if he could see into her soul. "Go ahead," he finally told her releasing her completely as he stepped back. "But be quick."

Miley nodded then backed away quickly. Once inside her room, she locked the bedroom door then whipped around and grabbed at a chair to shove under the door handle.

As the scrape and clunk of the wooden chair pressed up under the door, a swift hard knock made her screech. "What was that noise, Miley?" Orion called.

"Sorry. I just bumped into something…" Miley's voice shook slightly as she lied.

"Open the door." Orion growled, it was a scary noise and Miley was definitely not doing as he asked.

"Uh… no."

"Open the door!" He yelled as his fist pounded against the wood.

"No!" Miley screamed back as she scrambled across the room to look out her window. There had to be a way out of there and sure enough, the fire escape was going to be her way to safety.

She did not know this man and she wanted to get to Morgan… get to someone she was familiar with some place where this Orion or the man he had called, Diesel would not find her.

"Open this door Miley," Orion said slowly. Miley could tell he most likely had his teeth clenched in anger or frustration. "Or I'll break it down."

Miley scrambled out the window and onto the fire escape as fast yet as quiet as she could. As she raced down the sharp metal dug into the pads of her feet and she winced. However, within no time she was safely on the cool cement ground and running toward the building's front door.

By the time, she had made it around the building to the front door she could hear the most inhuman growl slash roar coming from the back of the building. It was angry or annoyed and downright ticked off. Worst of all it came from the man who must have just broken into her bedroom and was now glaring out the window for her.

Chapter 37

Miley slid her key to Morgan's apartment into the lock and twisted it quickly. She had raced up the staircase instead of using the elevator knowing that if Orion were to come down he would less likely look for her on them. Now, she stood one floor up in the hallway that lead to Morgan's apartment fumbling with the key and looking around her worriedly, anyone spotting her would think suspiciously of her.

When she was safely inside, she locked all three of the locks securely on Morgan's door then slid down it and let out a heavy breath.

"Who's there?" Morgan called into the darkness.

"Shhh… it's just me Morg," Miley whisper yelled, knowing that her friend would be armed with a baseball bat at the least.

Morgan flicked on the light, yawning and rubbed her tired eyes. "Miley?" Morgan replied. "What happen with the man you had in your room?"

"Ah… it's a long story. Can I hide here for the night?" Miley's voice was hushed and hurried.

"Sure." Morgan replied lightly. "We haven't had a sleep over in forever! Let's watch a movie."

"Great." Miley beamed pushing herself off the floor to walk over to the couch.

The two girls settled onto the couch and decided to watch a movie to settle them down before going to bed, even though Morgan had been sleeping prior.

It wasn't long until Morgan and Miley had fallen asleep curled up beside each other on the living room couch. The movie hadn't even been on for more than fifteen minutes. A loud banging made both girls shoot up from the couch screeching. "What was that?!" Morgan cried.

"Open up Miley! I know you're in there!" Orion's voice boomed through the door.

"That's the guy isn't it...?" Morgan hissed.

"Shh... I'm not here." Miley whispered as she raced through the apartment to hide in Morgan's bedroom.

Morgan groaned. She knew she needed to answer the door or the neighbors would be calling the police on her for the noise disturbance. Morgan let out a breath and rolled her eyes as she reached beside the couch and took a tight grip on her baseball bat.

"Quiet you'll wake the neighbors, I'm coming..." Morgan called back to Orion's yelling.

Morgan unlocked the two standard locks on her door but left the hefty chain lock in place as she slowly opened the door. "Who the heck do you think you are... pounding on my door in the middle of the night...?" Morgan began but soon lost her voice as she came face to face with the most handsome man she had ever met.

Why Miley had hid this man from her or why she was hiding from the gorgeous creature was beyond her and she knew she should have questioned it earlier.

"I know she's in here. I need to speak with Miley right now." Orion said stepping closer to the door.

Morgan gawked and her mouth opened and closed like a fish as she struggled to find the words to say. "I'm armed…" She muttered.

Orion rose an eyebrow and began to smirk, "Oh really."

"You better leave… she's not here." Morgan argued.

Orion's grin grew bigger on his delicious looking lips and Morgan knew instantly she was going to lose the battle. He reached forward and pressed a hand to the door. "I'll give you one last chance to let me in…," he said slowly.

"I can't do that…" Morgan swallowed down a hard lump in her throat as she tried to shove the door closed.

"Move, I don't want you to get hurt."

Before Morgan could do much to reach Orion shoved the door just slightly causing the chain to snap and when he had enough room he laced an arm around Morgan's waist and twirled her away from the door allowing himself enough room to get inside.

Pressing Morgan toward the wall he leaned down over her and breathed her in. "Now aren't you just adorable." He grinned.

Morgan blushed. She had been only in a short pair of shorts and a tank top. Now this man was looking at her as if she was the only water in a desert, and he was beyond thirsty.

"Thanks…" Morgan muttered shyly.

"Are you going to tell me where she is or do I need to search her out?" Orion questioned.

Morgan tried her best not to rat out her friend but within moments her arm raised on it's own accord and she pointed toward the bedroom where Miley had hidden.

"Thanks. I'll be back for you in a few moments," he grinned gently releasing her.

Morgan watched unmoving as the gorgeous mysterious man, which had been in Miley's room with her doing who knows what with her, walked across her home.

Chapter 38

The door to Morgan's bedroom swung open and Miley came out of the bathroom yawning. "Morgan, can we just…" she began, but quickly shut up by the man standing before her.

"You really think that running around the building can deter a dragon's nose?" Orion questioned.

Miley huffed and backed away from him as she spoke. "What did you do with Morgan?"

"That cute girl out there…" he asked amused, "she's fine."

"Morgan!" Miley screamed.

"She said yelling would wake the neighbors" Orion told her. "Do I need to cuff you to something… or?"

Letting the question hang in the air, Orion stepped toward Miley quickly collecting her wrist in his big palm. She shook her head no and pinched her eyes shut anxiously. "Please don't hurt me… please don't hurt Morgan." Her voice was nearly a whisper but Orion heard the words clearly.

He sighed, taking pity on the woman; he released her wrist and shook his head. "You may have annoyed me but trust me darling, I could not 'hurt' you if I wanted to live."

"Excuse me?"

"You heard me, I'm loyal to you. Your new mate is my alpha. I am loyal to him and so I am loyal to you." Orion told her. "But I won't let you run off, he'll be here soon and then you'll be free of me…" Orion said before adding "somewhat."

Orion nodded his head toward the door "let's go get your friend."

"Yeah… she's probably worried." Miley said quickly scurring around Orion and toward the door.

"Oh thank goodness," Morgan breathed as she snapped out of her confusion and rushed toward Miley wrapping her arms tightly around her.

"Ladies… it's late, why don't we head to bed?" Orion cleared his throat.

"Is he staying here?" Morgan whispered causing Orion to smirk and Miley to flush.

She nodded shyly "yeah I guess so."

"Well uh Mister…" Morgan began.

"Orion," Miley muttered at the same time as Orion himself spoke his name.

"What an amazing name." Morgan beamed. "You can have the couch."

Orion smirked even more than his normal one and shook his head "I'll be sleeping wherever she is. I'll take the floor if I need too."

Chapter 39

The girls slept side by side on Morgan's bed while Orion slept uncomfortably on the floor in the same room. When Miley awoke, she was relieved to think it was all just a horrible dream. She could smell the delicious scent of a home cooked breakfast as she sat up and padded across the floor.

"I had the strangest dream," she began as she walked out to the kitchen and could not believe her eyes.

"Oh you're up!" Morgan squeaked out in surprise. She was sitting on the counter with Orion between her legs. He pulled away only slightly and turned toward Miley with a grin.

"Morning," he grinned, "I was just getting to know your friend here…"

"Sure you were." Miley muttered skeptically.

"Miley it's not what you think…" Morgan tried to defend herself but Miley rose an eyebrow at her.

"Well, I'm going to go home and change." Miley groaned walking toward the door.

Orion looked toward Morgan and then back at Miley, struggling with a heavy decision to make. Then he quickly bolted toward the door. "Hey, I told you I have to stay with you until he gets here. It's not…"

"Well you seem a little occupied." Miley shrugged. "Anyway, I'm a big girl; I can take care of myself."

She yanked the door open and did not even wait for Orion to catch up. He was at a loss of what exactly to do. Stay with the girl, which he now has chosen as his mate or chase after his alpha's mate who is his responsibility.

Whipping around, Orion ran back toward the kitchen. "I need you to come up to Miley's apartment. I got to go after her…," he said quickly before adding a drawn out "please."

He kissed her forehead and turned around racing out into the hall to catch up with Miley. Luckily, she had nothing on his speed nor did she bother to run as he raced down the hall and found her standing casually before the elevator doors.

As the doors opened and Miley stepped inside, Orion did as well. She pressed the button to her floor and then turned to glare at him. "What is with you and my friend?" She questioned.

"Don't look at me like that." Orion rolled his eyes.

"You had her straddling you as you pinned her to the countertop." Miley snapped.

"What I do…" Orion began.

"Is my business too, when it includes my best friend," Miley interrupted. "And I don't think you should be dragging her into your mess of a life."

"Mess," Orion laughed. "You remember."

"I don't know what you are talking about." Miley rolled her eyes and looked away as the elevator door opened.

Stepping out and walking quickly, did not get her out of the situation though; Orion laughed and quickly caught pace with her. "You do!" He beamed. "Diesel's going to be so glad to hear that!"

"Listen here mister." Miley whipped around and pointedly jabbed a finger toward Orion as he dug into his pocket to begin calling Diesel. "You will not be telling him no such thing."

Orion's lip pulled into something that represented confusion as he cocked his head to the side and began to speak "and why not?" He questioned.

"What if I don't want this life, huh? Have you ever thought about that?" Miley hissed.

"You can't be serious!" he choked.

"Well maybe I am." Miley shrugged pushing a key into her door's lock. "I'm going inside and you… are going to leave. Stay away from Morgan."

"That's not quite how it's going to work." Orion huffed as he gently pushed Miley inside and stepped in behind her. With lightning like speed, he spun her around and pinned her to the wall. "I am going to take your friend back home with me, and you can't stop me. You on the other hand are going to behave for just another day until Diesel's flight gets in, then I'm going to turn you over to him."

Miley squirmed and tried her best to move but she knew she stood no chance against the man's strength.

"Let me go!" Miley snarled.

"Don't cause me any more problems."

He pushed up from the wall and walked across the room to slump down on the couch. Orion could tell Miley was contemplating an escape but was slightly afraid to act on it. He let her walk out of the room and into her bedroom alone.

Think fast, Miley reached for her cell phone and dialed Morgan's number. Whispering into the phone when Morgan answered Miley practically begged her friend to get out of the building and hide somewhere.

"Miley." Morgan sighed. "Why is it you were hiding this man from me? He's so …" Morgan sighed.

"No Morgan listen, please," Miley begged. "I have to get away from him and you do too. He's …" Miley thought what kind of words would help her to convince her friend when the word "dangerous," finally blurt out of her mouth.

"Dangerous?" Morgan laughed.

"If you don't go Morgan…" Miley whined, "I can't help what will happen but I am going to leave."

"You do what you have to do Miles. I'll be over in a bit; we'll go get dinner later." With that, Morgan hung up the phone.

"Miley?" Orion called from the other room causing Miley to turn toward the noise and glare.

"Leave me alone!" Miley snapped.

Orion chuckled.

Soon there was a knocking on Miley's door and she eagerly ran toward the opposite side of the house trying to answer the door before Orion could get up.

"I'll answer that." Orion said standing up.

"Nope, thanks." Miley said quickly.

She yanked the door open and Morgan smiled back at her as she pushed herself inside. "Hey Miles."

"I asked you to…" Miley muttered.

"I know Miles. Run…" Morgan groaned, "I just did not listen," she beamed as she looked away. "Hey Orion."

"Hey darling," he grinned. Standing up he walked toward Morgan with open arms and Miley watched dumb founded as Morgan wrapped herself into Orion's arms.

It had only been one night in her apartment and they had not even said much to each other. Let alone talk! Now the two were lovey dovey?

"Gah!" Miley snorted then stomped across the apartment. She flopped herself on to the free couch and flicked on the television.

"I'll get it!" Miley stretched standing up the movie she had chosen had been too boring and the company wasn't good company when the two began to start smooching.

"Well hello." The man on the other side of the door grinned pressing the door open. Miley turned her head around and found Orion was rising to his feet with a satisfied grin.

Chapter 40

"Go away?" Miley asked turning around.

"Who is he?!" Morgan blurt, trying not to screech too loudly.

"What?" Miley huffed facing her friend.

"You go awol, telling me you're going on a work trip and I come to visit once you get back and find a hunk like him in your house and another knocking on your door!"

Diesel chuckled. Miley turned around glaring. "He is nobody," she growled watching Diesel's satisfying smirk fade. He had been dressed in an impressive pair of dark wash jeans that hung low on his hips and a black button up dress shirt, which made him look drool worthy. His bright violet eyes had been slightly washed out by the darkness of his shirt and his face held light stubble across his jaw.

Diesel stepped forward into the apartment fully and shut the door behind him with a smile on his lips. Extending his hand he said, "Hello, my name is Diesel McBride and you are?"

"Morgan…" Morgan muttered with a slight giggle as she grabbed his hand. She leaned toward Miley with bright eyes, "He's so hot!" she said in a hushed whisper.

"He is not!" Miley hissed back at the same time as Orion growled.

"I am Miley's best friend." Morgan cooed. "Are you her new boy toy? It's about time she got over Toby…" Morgan continued.

"MORGAN!" Miley scolded.

"He's your soon to be ex!" Morgan snapped back. "So who is he?" she said pointing over Miley's shoulder toward Diesel.

"I told you Morgan… He's no…" Miley begun but Diesel interrupted.

"I'm her boyfriend."

Orion chuckled and sat back down watching the cat fight before him.

"You are not!" Miley scolded turning toward Diesel angrily. With both hands, she reached up and pushed him away from Morgan. "In the other room NOW," Miley hissed, "before you cause more damage!"

"What?" Diesel groaned but he let Miley push him wherever she wanted to go.

"I have to take a shower and get ready to go. I have some plans," she said with one final shove. "If you're going to be here then stay in here until I leave Then you can watch television or something until I get back as long as you don't talk to Morgan, although, I would prefer if you left."

"Miley," Diesel protested as she shut the door behind her leaving him in her bedroom.

"So!" Morgan cooed stepping up to Miley as she stormed into the kitchen for a drink.

"It's not what you think Mor," Miley groaned.

"Oh come on Miles…, he's cute." Morgan chuckled. Orion growled and walked up to Morgan wrapping an arm around her shoulder.

"Who's cute?" He questioned.

Morgan rolled her eyes. "Go on, it's girl talk time." Morgan giggled slapping Orion's arm playfully as he grunted and walked toward the bedroom where Miley had stashed Diesel.

"Where do you think you are going?" Miley snapped walking after Orion.

"You know where I'm going." He replied leaving her still fuming.

"Look Morgan. If you want to go out to dinner later, I need to get in a shower before we leave… please excuse me."

"Fine! I'll wait out here!" Morgan called back with a huff and reached in Miley's fridge getting her own bottle of water. "Send the boys back out here would you?"

Miley stormed past Diesel and Orion with a pissed off expression across her face and straight into her bathroom. She closed the door and pulled off her clothes fiercely. When the water was warm enough Miley slid inside and sighed. This man was going to destroy everything.

The bathroom door creaked open and Miley stopped rubbing her hands over her hair "Morgan… I'll be out in a minute you could not wait out there and watch a movie or something?"

"I'm not your bubbly blond friend." Diesel spoke, his voice once again thick with a strange accent that she had noticed a few of the people on the island speaking with.

"GET OUT!" She cried as Diesel pressed a hand to the shower curtain.

She looked over at Diesel's face on the other side of the shower curtain. She did not expect him to be well… naked.

"Well love, I just wanted to see you with your hair down…" Diesel teased. He pushed his leg into the tub and slowly tantalizingly stepped inside.

"Get. Out. Now!" Miley screeched and before she could step out of the shower, Diesel's hands pinned her to the wall.

"You look amazing with your hair down." He smirked as his eyes roamed down Miley's body.

He slid one hand down Miley's body, while the other kept her from leaving. "Get out." Miley huffed pathetically.

"You want me to leave?" Diesel asked with a grin.

"Yes?" Miley murmured. Her voice was filled with uncertainty.

"I don't think you want me to leave…" Diesel purred as he leaned toward her and pressed his lips to hers.

Miley could not help it. The way their bodies merged together and the way their lips moved with one another was magical. She could feel herself loving this man. She could see a future with this man. Then it all came crashing down once again. "Miley?" Morgan's voice called back toward Miley's bedroom.

"Get out now." Miley breathed heavily. She was panting from their kiss and her lips were plump and slightly swollen. "and maybe I will spare your balls from being crushed with a hammer," she finished with as she shoved against Diesel's well defined chest.

"Well fine then." Diesel chuckled stepping away of the shower and wrapping a towel around his waist. "Maybe lock the door next time or well… maybe we can enjoy ourselves a bit longer." The man was so irresistible, Miley could not stand it. She sighed and pressed her hand onto the shower faucet. She had to get dressed before she ran out there and jumped him.

Miley finished her shower and stepping out it seemed strangely quiet. Diesel was nowhere in sight. Miley sighed happily maybe he had left; well that's what she hoped for until she heard Morgan's rapid voice going on about something.

Miley dressed quickly and stormed toward the sound of her friend speaking. She just knowing that it was Diesel she was talking too. "Yeah well… Miley's one hard nut to crack," she heard Morgan sigh before adding "it took Toby like a year just to get her to go out on a date with him and then he went and…"

"Morgan!" Miley screeched.

"Oh uh… Miles… we were just" She paused.

"Talking right," Miley snorted. "I'm leaving," she huffed and continued past her friend and the men toward the door. She had pulled on a pair of boot cut designer jeans and a designer bright red tank top with a black leather coat over top. Her red stilettos slapped across the hard wood flooring as she walked.

"Miley, come on…" Morgan called after she pushed from the couch and took chase. Diesel and Orion stood slowly making their way behind the pair. "Hey…" Morgan pleaded, "We were just talking," she tried to reason with her friend but Miley was still angry.

"I don't want you to talk to him… I want him to go away." Miley hissed. "I don't want you to talk to either of them."

"I told you, my love. I am not going away." Diesel said stepping up beside Miley and grasping her hand.

"Let go of me!" she scolded stepping away.

"Look. I am going to have a girl's day with my friend here. If you want to talk with me later..." Miley snorted as she locked her house door. She was going to make sure that Diesel and Orion did not get back inside.

"Would you mind if I joined?" Diesel asked.

Morgan looked as if she wanted to say something but Miley beat her too it. "No you can't!"

"Miley, be reasonable." Morgan whispered which made Diesel's disappointment fade slightly. "What about him…" Morgan nodded slightly toward Orion.

Miley grabbed her friend by the hand and stormed down the corridor to the elevator. "He's not coming with us, neither of them are." Miley finally said as they made their way to the doorman.

"Miss Tanner," the doorman called joyously too happy for the time of the day.

Miley smiled and came up with a quick plan; leaning in she caught Howard in a hug before pulling him close and whispering to him, "these me that are following us… don't let them back in the building. They have been following us and it's creeping me out," Miley whimpered slightly for effect and pulled away from the doorman.

His face turned into a sneer and he stepped in before Orion and Diesel. "Excuse me, do you mind if I speak with you both over here a moment?"

Diesel's face faltered but he quickly covered it up with a straight, emotionless, and nearly scary looking one. "Miley." Morgan shook her head before speaking up. "Howard, leave the man alone. He's just a love sick puppy." Morgan smiled.

Diesel turned toward the doorman and nodded stiffly before walking off with him toward the security office. Orion stood stone still struggling to on which direction to go.

"Miley say something!" Morgan hissed.

"Fine," Miley huffed, "Howard let him be. Come on puppy," she commanded.

Diesel smiled genuinely, nodded to Howard, and then jogged back toward the girls as Orion breathed a sigh of relief then took up pace behind them. Morgan smirked and gripped tighter to her friend's hand, "come on let's go."

Once inside a large cab, Morgan huffed over at her friend before scooting over letting Diesel and Orion inside. "What's your deal Miley, this man is totally head over heels for you?" Morgan whispered to her friend.

Miley pinched the bridge of her nose and let out a slow breath. "I can't…" Miley paused trying to think of what she would say about the strange first meeting. "He's been nothing but a controlling dick." Miley said in a hushed voice.

"And you started sleeping with him anyway?" Morgan asked confusedly. She too was whispering but Diesel cocked his head slightly at the sound of Miley's screeching voice.

Neither of the girls knew that Diesel and Orion, could hear even their slightest whisper nor did they know that the screeching was like a knife stabbing into their brains; flat out too loud.

"I'm not sleeping with him!"

Diesel smiled. "That would be fun," he smirked.

"Interesting," Orion murmured.

Diesel growled.

"You broke into my apartment," Miley yelled glaring at Orion. "And you," she snorted turning her eyes toward Diesel, "I haven't ever had sex with you!"

"I did not." Orion shrugged "You left the door open."

Miley shook her head at the annoying man.

"Okay…" Morgan said slowly. "Well…" she paused and looked over to Diesel then back at Miley before whispering, "You should."

Diesel and Orion both chuckled and Miley nearly died of embarrassment. Even the cab driver nearly choked on his own air at Morgan's words. "Well, thank you Morgan." Diesel flit his eyes to Morgan with a grin. "I have been trying to get her attention for a while now."

Chapter 41

The entire girls' day, Morgan was trying to get Miley to at least consider giving Diesel a chance and Miley adamantly claimed it would never happen. Diesel tagged along and kept his mouth quiet for the most part. While Orion hung on Morgan's every word doing anything he could to touch her skin.

Both enjoyed watching the two girls get pampered. Diesel had brought them out to lunch and enjoyed watching as Miley received massages. He fought his beast, shoving him back down, wishing he was the one whose hands were rubbing Miley.

After Miley and Morgan had finished their day, the girls hugged. "Diesel, you're such a sweet guy." Morgan cooed hugging him as well. "I really hope you can convince Miley to give you a chance."

She turned toward Orion whom was now glaring over at Diesel. "Mind walking me home?" A smile grew on Orion's lips as he gripped Morgan's hand and together they began to walk away.

Miley snorted. "Bye, Morgan. See you later."

"Enjoy yourselves." Morgan smirked as she walked down the hall to her own apartment. "I know we will." Morgan was something else; she wore Miley out just listening to her ramble.

Miley turned to Diesel. He had followed the girls up and now Miley was unsure of how to get rid of him.

"Give me a chance." Diesel plead as he gently placed a hand on Miley's arm, "please."

It was getting late and Miley was getting tired. She slumped against wall. Sighing she knew what she had to do. "Do you have a place to stay?" she asked.

"No. I hadn't planned this whole trip out. I had men searching the city for you. Orion was suppose to bring you back…" he began, "but you insisted…" Diesel's words hung and he stared at her pleadingly.

Miley sighed then pushed the key into her door and turned it. The apartment was dim from the fading light outside.

Pushing the door and stepping inside she turned and stared at the man who seemed a little beat. "Come on," she sighed, "you can stay here for now."

Diesel smiled softly and stepped into the apartment. "You hungry?" She asked.

Diesel's shoulders slumped and his head hung low, looking up at her through his lashes he nodded, "yeah… sure."

"I'll call for pizza," Miley said turning around and walking into the kitchen.

"It'll be here in about twenty minutes." Miley called out when she turned around she squeaked. "Oh!"

Diesel stood hovering just behind her. "Do I really bother you?" he asked slowly.

"I can't do this." Miley said with a slight whimper pushing gently on Diesel's chest.

"Why?" Diesel questioned.

"Please… I can't…" Miley looked away, she could not look up into his defeated beautiful eyes. A single tear trickled down her cheek.

Diesel sighed and pushed from his position backing away slightly. "What has he done to you?" He murmured.

Miley turned to look up at Diesel through her thick lashes. Diesel did not seem to be looking for an answer because he began again "I'll change your opinion."

"Please leave." Miley whispered. She had changed so quickly.

"Miley." Diesel said slowly stepping in her direction. In her hand Diesel assumed was what most human called a cell phone. He sighed.

Miley looked up anxiously. "Get out of my house Diesel."

"Hand me the phone love." Diesel said.

"No." Miley replied tightening her grip ever so slightly.

"Front desk, how may I help you…" the person on the other side of the phone line asked.

"I …" Miley began.

Diesel could tell the closer he got the more confused Miley became. "Hand over the phone, Miley." He said slowly. Miley took a step back watching Diesel as his predatory stare bore into her. She knew this man was different, she could remember the strange things to do with dragons and Diesel being one of them.

He lived on an island filled with strange happenings. He had those tantalizingly beautiful violet eyes and his touch sparked a fire within her. Miley still hadn't fully understood if she was dreaming up everything that had happened on the island or not. Everything was swirling within her, even though she knew whole heartedly that everything was real.

Diesel is a dragon. A beautiful massive creature with bright violet eyes and she had been kidnapped by another which had shipped her back here and asked for her to send in all the photos she had not actually taken of the dragons in exchange for a large sum of money.

"Don't take another step…" Miley warned.

"Ma'am, are you alright?" the person on the phone asked more nervously this time.

Diesel knew this was a losing game. If he wanted to stop her call then he had to take quick action. Miley wasn't distracted but he could not take the chance.

Bending his knees slightly Diesel launched himself toward Miley and grabbed the phone straight from her hand before she could comprehend saying another word into it.

"I'm sorry wrong number." Diesel said into the phone as he clicked it shut.

Miley's eyes were wide and she stared at the man before her. She began to open her mouth but Diesel spoke. "Please don't scream." He asked.

He could tell by Miley's eyes she was beginning to panic. They darted around the room, she turned on her heal and raced toward her room. Diesel took a few quick strides grabbing Miley by the waist and pulling her to a stop before twisting her around to face him. "Please quit doing that." He said softly.

"Let me go!" Miley yelled pushing away from Diesel.

"Calm down. I'm not going to hurt you… I just…" Diesel began. With his senses on high alert Diesel learned quickly when it came to this girl, so when her knee came up to knee him in the groin, Diesel caught it with his hand.

"Hey… Don't you realize how much that would hurt?" He growled softly amusement clearly on his face as Miley was caught off guard.

His fingers slowly traced over the thin jean material. "Fine!" She huffed.

"And if you ever wish to have children… then I would highly suggest against it." Diesel's lips were pulled into a smirk and Miley's mouth opened wide.

"Excuse me?!" she gaped at him.

"You heard me, sweetheart. You will miss those items if you ever want to have children… me well, I would like as many as you would let me have."

Miley scowled "What do you want Diesel? I am not interested in having children with you. I am not interested in going back to your 'island' with you cither."

Diesel frowned "Can we work on that?"

"Let go of me and stay back. I guess we can talk then," she sighed.

"Thank you." Diesel grinned. Deep down inside he was giddy. Talking was good.

"Did you bring my things?" She asked.

"Uh…" Diesel answered.

"You left them?" she frowned.

"Well, I wasn't quite worried about clothing when I had my clan out searching for you and we had a war going on." He shrugged.

"Oh," Miley replied stepping further away from the tall gorgeous man before her.

"Love, I did not take a plane." Diesel's lips curled up into a smirk. There was so much that she did not know about him yet.

"What do you mean," Miley frowned. "How did you get here then?"

"You don't know?" Diesel asked.

"Know what?" Miley asked sitting down on the couch curling a blanket around her as she pretended she was clueless.

"Love… what do you remember about the island?" Diesel asked curiously. The island had mysterious properties and had the ability to hide the secrets from visitors minds but he had a feeling that it had chosen Miley remembered everything.

Miley wiggled and then looked up at Diesel with those smothering violet eyes once again. "I remember everything." Miley stated "I won't tell. Is that why you came here?"

"Love…" Diesel smiled softly. "I am exactly like those creatures you saw. I am their alpha. Their leader. I am the strongest and biggest dragon within miles of our home. You have to realize that. I am crazy for you." Diesel said stepping around the couch and sitting down beside Miley. He hung his head holding it up with the palms of his hands and his elbows on his knees.

He looked sad. Miley could not help but feel the urge to sooth him. "I'm sorry," she said quietly.

A buzz interrupted her words and Miley stood up. "Pizza's here," she beamed.

"Meat lovers, coke, and breadsticks" The man said holding out the food to Miley.

"Yeah, thanks," she said handing the delivery man the money and closing the door. "Come on Diesel, food's here."

Diesel stood and made his way to the kitchen. Accepting the food from Miley he made his way slowly over to the table. "How about we watch a movie?" Miley asked walking up beside him with a smile.

"Sure." Diesel replied as he followed Miley.

After their dinner was done, Miley had put the food away. Diesel walked up behind her gently placing a hand on her arm. "Can I show you now?" he asked quietly.

"Not now." Miley yawned. "I'm tired. I want to get some sleep. I have an appointment tomorrow." Diesel could tell earlier that Morgan was tiring. He sighed, teaching Miley more about himself and the new life he wanted her in would have to come tomorrow.

"Sure." Diesel sighed.

His voice was soft and thick with that same strange accent from before. For some reason it seemed to come and go as he spoke to different people. Sighing Miley nodded her head.

"You can sleep in the guest room," she groaned. Miley had been meaning to get another roommate but had yet to find one acceptable enough.

That wasn't what Diesel really was hoping for but he would accept it. Miley showed Diesel down the hall to the guest room.

Pushing the door open, Miley rolled her eyes. "Here you go. I better not find you in my room again," she hissed the last part angrily.

Diesel could tell earlier that day that Miley wasn't quite mad about his appearance in her room in fact she seemed quite interested. Her heartbeat had speed up ever so slightly and he could smell the lust pouring out of her like sweat.

As he squeezed past Miley, he grinned and leaned closer to her. Miley shied away slightly and ducked her head sucking in a breath. Diesel sucked in a deep breath and closed his eyes, purring slightly, "mmm, too bad. I bet we could have a good time."

That was where he had left her. Miley's face had turned a bright red heat flushing her and she scurried away as Diesel began to strip down to just boxers.

Chapter 42

Miley did not know what to do. She had tried her best to get the guy to leave her alone. She could not take another heartbreak from a too tempting hot guy. What if this guy turned into another Toby and found someone new. For some reason, Miley did not know if she could quite handle that.

She had to scurry away before she caught sight of the sexy man stripping his clothing for bed. She knew for sure, she could not handle that! Miley had taken to her room and though she could not quite get to sleep. She had rolled around for hours. Eventually, Miley just grunted as she grabbed a blanket and stomped into the other room.

Diesel hadn't been able to sleep as he had suspected. Around three a.m. he found his way to the kitchen to grab a drink trying to calm his restless body.

Yawning, Miley stumbled into the kitchen, her sight was fuzzy from sleep and she did not expect to see him standing there. Nope, definitely not. Without paying any attention what-so-ever Miley walked right into Diesel's hard chest.

"Owf," she grunted stumbling back. "Oh! Diesel, I'm ah…" she muttered.

Miley was going to say sorry for walking into the man's chest but when her eyes finally became used to the light which Diesel snapped on and she found him standing before her looking more stunning than ever before. Her eyes trailed down his tight chest, to his strong abdominal muscles all the way down to…

"Ahem…" Diesel chuckled softly. "I sure don't mind if you stare my love but I would prefer if you did not look so …" he paused trying to find the right word. Not finding what he wanted he just simply shook his head, "sexy when you stared," he smirked.

Miley's eyes snapped up to Diesel's violet ones. "I would never," she snorted side stepping him and grabbing a water bottle from the fridge.

"Oh, but you would." Diesel smirked. "Could not sleep?" He asked curiously.

"No." Miley yawned, looking up at Diesel with her droopy brown eyes. Mesmerized, Diesel's thoughts drifted off to what a mix of their eye colors would bring out in any future children. "I was going to put on a movie."

"Oh. Do you mind if I joined you?" Diesel asked yawning slightly. He had been overly tired from the trip here and he has yet to have enough time with Miley to rejuvenate himself.

"Uh…" Miley said tentatively looking around the house and then nervously back up at Diesel, "if you stay on your side of the couch."

Diesel's laughter filled the small space of the kitchen and Miley smiled. She did not know exactly why but it was the most beautiful sound she had ever heard in her life. "I get to pick." he chuckled as he raced across the room before Miley could move.

"Hey!" She cried out but only moved at a third of Diesel's speed. Though, he had been tired the beast within Diesel would always be able to sustain more speed than the smaller human girl. "It's my house!"

Diesel huffed. "But I am the guest."

"And that's not my fault your free to leave." Miley shook her head. She could not get past this stranger here in her home who felt more like a long lost friend.

Diesel really did not care what movie they watched as long as Miley was happy. Instead, he just slumped his shoulders in fake defeat and wandered over to the couch. Miley quickly grabbed what movie she had obviously been already thinking off, popped it into the player, and made her way back over to the couch.

"That is my spot," she puffed slapping her hands on her hips and in the process accidently dropping the blanket which was covering her.

"Ah…" Diesel murmured. His eyes were stuck somewhere other than up at hers and his hands desperately wanted to reach out to her soft skin.

"Oh!" Miley jumped slightly grabbing frantically for the fallen blanket. She had forgotten that she had gone to bed in just a tiny pair of underwear and a camisole. Pulling the blanket back around her, she tried to avoid Diesel's intense gaze.

"Sorry," he muttered out quickly moving his eyes up to hers. "I did not mean to stare. You're just so beautiful." Diesel breathed softly.

"Ah… no... I'm not." Miley replied. She curled herself into the far side of the couch then pulled the blanket tightly around her.

Diesel raised an eyebrow. He had found a bit of information that Miley would never have released otherwise and he was going to use it to his advantage.

Though they were so far apart on opposite sides of the couch, both seemed to unconsciously move closer. Half way through the movie, Miley was curled up beside Diesel, her head curled against his chest and sleep had over taken her. Diesel though took a slight bit longer to fall asleep. He simply watched over Miley with a soft smile playing on his lips, twirling his fingers gingerly though her hair, which had fallen down from her messy pony tail; until his eyes slipped shut.

Chapter 43

"So, you took my advice?" Miley's eyes shot open and she frantically tried to get away from the warm figure that was next to her. Finding a heavy warm lump wrapped around her she pushed at it, looking around for the source of the disturbance.

"Huh?" she mumbled.

"I spot this hot guy in your house and when we go out you swear up and down you're not sleeping with him and what happens… I come to make sure you look good for your meeting with Toby and find you curled up with him? I can't even look at you." Morgan's face was stern but her eyes filled with something that was more along the lines of laughter. She had tried hard not to laugh when she caught her friend curled up against the hot man whom she had yet to know much about. She was not really mad just amused.

"What?" Miley grunted as she pushed the lump away from her. She struggled from the couch and ended up getting tangled in the blanket and toppling over.

"Well," Morgan mused. "I haven't caught you like that with a man in forever," she smirked.

"We did not do anything!" Miley screeched racing into her room. Diesel missing Miley by his side yawned and stretched as he slowly stood up.

"Well hello…" Morgan smiled broadly, as her eyes trailed down Diesel's taught abs to his black boxer clad bottom.

Diesel's eyes widened and he turned to look at Morgan. Covering himself with the blanket he bowed his head and made his way down the hall. He tapped softly on Miley's bedroom door.

"Miley."

"Go away," she cried.

"Awe, come on beautiful…" Diesel whined.

"Fine!" Miley grunted and opened the bedroom door "what do you want Diesel… to make my life more embarrassing?"

"We did nothing wrong, Miley," he said softly as he pushed against the door.

"Just go away," she sobbed softly.

"Come here princess." Diesel replied as he spread his hands out wide.

Miley shook her head but slowly leaned into him anyway. She felt comforted by his presence but she did not say anything. Diesel's calloused fingers stroked gently across Miley's back, while his other hand entwined in her hair. "You should wear your hair down sometime," he said softly as he tugged at it.

"Why do you keep chasing me?" she said softly.

"I told you, I want you. You're beautiful and feisty. You're a tease. I'm head-over-heels for you." Diesel said smoothing his hand down her cheek and tipping her head up to him.

"But why me?" Miley murmured. "I'm broken. You don't want a woman like me," she cried softly.

"Again… You're beautiful and amazing. I would be beyond honored even just to get a kiss from you."

"You would want to kiss me?" Miley muttered.

Diesel nodded.

"You are not human, are you?" Miley stated.

"I am all the man you would ever need and so much more." Diesel's words were husky and again that strange accent loomed between them.

Miley moaned slightly as Diesel pressed his body into hers.

He slowly gripped onto Miley's hips and pulled her in closer. She had yet to dress and he wanted to claim her right then. He was struggling to contain the beast, which desperately was trying to get off his chain.

It was strange and foreign for him to not shift on a daily basis but since he had been here in New York, he had to keep himself in check. The land here was too occupied by humans and it would be too easy to let it slip.

Not being able to contain himself any more Diesel leaned down and pressed his lips to Miley's. Stunned for a moment she stumbled backward, but Diesel gripped tighter to her hips continuing to follow her back toward the wall without breaking their kiss.

Soon Miley's lips began to move with him and a soft moan escaped her lips. He grunted in approval as Miley's fingers found their way to his hair. He pulled back slightly and kissed his way down to her jaw and back up.

The door suddenly burst open and the spell was broken causing Miley to frantically push Diesel away. "Oh uh… I figured… um let me know when you need my help." Morgan mumbled as she slowly shut the door.

"Crap," Miley groaned.

"Miley." Diesel began but she was already pushing him away.

"Go get dressed," she stated simply.

Diesel nodded his head and made his way to the guest room.

Morgan had returned later after Miley was ready. She had picked out something super sexy in a 'make him want me back' type way for Miley's meeting. "Ooo…" Morgan screeched this is the perfect dress."

"I can't wear that!" Miley complained. It was totally not a strictly 'I mean business' type dress it was more of a 'come and get me… I'm crazy desperate' type dress, Miley thought.

"Oh yes you can and I am going to tell you why… that boy toy you have in the other room is going to go with you as your buffer." Morgan told her firmly wiggling the tiny black dress back and forth.

"No Morgan… he can't." Miley whined.

"He's crazy for you. He is going to have you… eventually I just know it." Morgan giggled.

"Exactly, why he can't go. Look at that dress. He's going to …"

Morgan cut in holding her finger up to Miley's lips. "He's going to struggle not to jump you right in front of Toby and Toby would never even consider trying something… with that hunk beside you," Morgan assured. "Now get dressed."

Miley sighed. Morgan did know best when it came to this type thing, or at least better than Miley did. Grabbing the dress Miley groaned as she made her way to the bathroom once again. At first she had tried to pull the dress on with the underwear she had been wearing but neither the bra nor the underwear was going to work.

"Ah come on!" Miley groaned as she wrapped a towel around her body and stomped back into her bedroom.

"What's the problem now?" Morgan huffed.

"Nothing," Miley snorted as she dug through her closet drawers. Finally, finding a sufficient pair of underwear and close enough matching strapless bra she patted her way back into the bathroom.

"O" Morgan's lips curled up in a slight grin and she laughed quietly watching her friend leave.

Morgan slipped from the room quickly rushing down the hall to find Diesel and Orion talking amongst together. She was going to inform Diesel that he was going to be going with Miley. "Diesel," Morgan called.

Orion growled and she looked over at him curiously.

"Oh… Hey uh… Megan was it?" Diesel asked his eyebrows furrowing as he looked up from Orion to Morgan.

"Uh… no it's Morgan, but that's irrelevant right now. I need you to get something oh… wait nope you look super sexy." Orion's gaze snapped over at Diesel as he growled. "Good," she clapped her hands together and turned to go back to Miley's room.

"Hey what's going on?" Diesel asked confused as stood and followed her.

"Oh… I just came to tell you that you're going with Miley to make her jealous ex." Morgan said as if it was nothing, waving her hand dismissively before walking away.

Diesel shrugged. He would have to ask Miley about it later but currently he just would finish cleaning up the living room and talking to Orion while they waited. The television was one of the many an amazing invention they talked about investing in. Nothing like they had on the island.

Morgan returned to the room just as Miley was coming out. She could not help but smile devilishly. "Oh he's going to go crazy!" Morgan squealed.

"Yeah, maybe," Miley shrugged as she turned herself around in the full length bedroom mirror.

"I mean your man out there…" Morgan giggled as she pushed her friend down in a chair to do her hair. "Now sit we still have an hour before you have to leave…"

Miley groaned. She wasn't quite sure she wanted Diesel to go 'crazy' over her. Yet, she was satisfied and partially confident that Toby's jaw would drop. She tried to rest while Morgan did her hair, but she kept wiggling in her place anxious to get up and find out what Diesel and Orion was doing in the other room.

"Hold still," Morgan snapped.

"But I don't want them out there by themselves." Miley complained.

"Fine!" Morgan huffed flinging the brush down and stomping from the room. Moments later she came back with Diesel and Orion in tow. "Sit," she demanded.

Diesel looked back at her not wanting to listen to the command. Who was she to demand anything of him? Then his eyes traveled across the room to a semi shocked beautiful Miley and he nearly fell onto the bed.

"Wow." He breathed.

"Yeah now just wait until I'm done with her." Morgan replied grabbing the brush and shoving it through Miley's hair.

Orion on the other hand had happily agreed to obey Morgan's demands. He sat down beside Diesel offering a gentle slap on the back.

Twenty minutes later, Miley's hair was pulled up into a swooping braid across the top of her head. Small strands cascaded out of the braid refusing to abide by Morgan's strict placement. Morgan stepped away allowing Diesel to have a full view as Miley stood up and patted across the room. "You look…" Diesel mouthed the air just barely escaping his lips as he spoke.

"Do I look good?" Miley swirled around.

Diesel found Miley's beauty mesmerizing and she made it hard for him to breath. He wanted nothing more than to ravage her. His eyes scrolled down her, from the tips of her chocolate colored hair past her semi-bare shoulders and down the length of her dress. He smiled approvingly.

"Yep, he definitely likes it." Orion nodded.

Morgan gave Miley a slight push. "Do not and I repeat, do not, mess up that hair until you get home."

Morgan grabbed hold of Orion's hand and began to drag him out of the room before Miley could really take her eyes away from Diesel. He had been studying her dress or at least the body beneath the tiny black dress and it made her blush. "So what do you think… will it make Toby feel jealous?" Miley asked cautiously.

"Who's Toby?" Diesel nearly growled as his body lunged up and he playfully pinned Miley to the wall.

Miley's cheeks flamed and she looked up at him through her dark lashes. "He's my ex. Ah… I have to meet him to discuss a few things…" Miley said nervously.

"And I'm coming…" Diesel let the words say what he really meant. It wasn't really a question but a statement one that he was hoping she wouldn't try and disobey. He just could not let her out of his sight looking so sexy. He pulled back slightly looking down at the small black dress again. It had large slits along Miley's right side showing off her tanned silky skin in multiple spots, almost looking like there was nothing beneath, and if there was she did a good job at hiding it. He growled slightly as he let his fingers roam over the bare skin of her hip.

"Yeah… that's what I heard," Miley said slowly. She was finding it terribly hard to concentrate with this man so … all over her.

"You look … words can't describe what I think about you right now." Diesel said in a low rumble of satisfaction.

"Thanks," Miley smiled softly before ducking beneath Diesel's out stretched arm and making her way down the hall. She had been extremely nervous about seeing Toby again, but maybe with Diesel by her side, things would be alright. She was beginning to like his presence.

Chapter 44

Diesel protectively placed an arm around Miley's waist as they walked down to the lobby. "Mrs. Tanner?" Howard, the doorman, asked. "I thought…"

Miley smiled over at Howard. "Sorry Howard, I changed my mind. He's fine for now."

"Okay ma'am, let me know if anything changes." Howard glared at Diesel.

Diesel tipped his head in a nod to Howard but pulled Miley closer to again. "Is that where we're going today?"

"Yep," Miley grunted. It had been a mistake to get in a relationship with Toby so quickly. They had married the day after she graduated from college and it had been the biggest mistake ever. Not even a week in and she had caught Toby cheating and being that she was so blinded she hadn't made him sign a pre-nuptial and now Toby was trying to take everything from her.

The divorce papers were issued and Morgan had helped Miley to get the apartment within a week of the incident but still even with the lawyers help they hadn't settled everything.

To make matters worse, the home her parents had given them for their honeymoon was given to Miley's sister.

"When were you planning on telling me?" Diesel asked, Miley looked up at him slightly embarrassed.

"I was hoping I did not need too, it slipped my mind. Toby ah... just..." Diesel sighed.

"He frustrates you," Diesel stated.

Miley nodded. "Well at least I can propose when it's all settled." Diesel shrugged and then chuckled when Miley's face flushed.

Shaking her head Miley began to wave for a taxi. "What are you doing?" Diesel asked.

"Hailing a taxi," Miley's eyebrows furrowed as Diesel pulled her hand down.

"Why don't we take my car?" he asked casually.

"You have a car here?" Miley asked confusedly.

"I rented one. Did not know how long it would take to get you to come back with me..." Diesel said slowly.

"I'm not going back with you," Miley frowned.

"We'll talk about that later," Diesel said as he gave the apartment's concierge a ticket.

He was back quickly with a slick black sports car. "Wow," Miley cooed. "I like it. Wait... You got the concierge to park a car for you and you don't even live here?" she questioned.

"Well... a large tip helps," he shrugged and opening the door for Miley. Once she slid inside, Diesel closed the door and walked around to the other side. "Anyway... don't you have a car?" Diesel asked as he slid into the driver's side.

"Oh uh... long story," Miley laughed nervously. "Anyway... head to 7625 Main Street," Miley stated.

Diesel could tell that was a sore subject. The ride to the address, which Miley had provided, was silent, but not overly tense. Miley seemed to be continually thinking about something anxiously, while Diesel followed the directions of the navigation device the rental sales man had showed him how to use.

When they finally showed up at the tall stone building, Miley's eyes stared nervously out the window, "crap…," she groaned.

"Are you alright?" Diesel asked as he reached for the door handle.

"Don't!" Miley cried out. Diesel turned and raised an eyebrow at her and for a moment, it was silent. He was about to ask when Miley spoke again nervously, "He's watching," she whispered.

"I'll make it good, love," Diesel smiled.

"I owe you." Miley tried desperately to crack a smile but it just wouldn't come.

"I'll get the door. Just follow my lead beautiful," Diesel told her as he pushed the door open and climbed out.

The sports car's door glided upward slowly making Toby watch on in search for Miley. Toby loved cars and it was hard for him to ignore the slick black Audi 9. It by far would be one of the cars he would buy if he had the choice but it wasn't cheap.

He shook his head. Of course, it would be a good lookin' guy, in a casual yet designer outfit, which would be getting out not some hot chick. Tempted to look away, Toby continued to search for Miley.

He was considering asking her to forget the divorce, heck she was better off financially then most of the other girls he had met lately and he sure was interested in the money.

Though the time he spent with Miley's sister, Rebecca, well that was good, but he could not convince her to marry him until he got rid of Miley. Besides he already had her hooked, he got her pregnant. It was more than he could do with Miley. The bitch wanted to be on birth control. She had told him they should strengthen their relationship first. Little did Miley know, two of Rebecca's children were his spawn.

It was when the man walked around to the other side and opened the passenger door that Toby really took a second look. The woman slid out and Toby felt himself grow angry. The man pulled a beautiful looking Miley, which by the way was dressed to kill in a sexy tight black dress. Then he pulled her into his side and kissed her lips. They pulled away from each other and continued toward the concierge.

After the slick black car pulled away, Toby watched as the man and Miley walked up toward the building. Toby sighed and backed away from the window. "Toby?" a whiny female voice asked.

"In hear Lola." Toby smiled.

"Ah… your lawyer is waiting in the conference room. I guess Miley's on her way up," Lola smiled sweetly.

"Lola, I need your help today. Would you mind coming with me?" Toby asked.

"Oh!" Lola giggled. "I would love too." Clapping happily, Lola bounced toward Toby grabbing his arm happily.

"Off," Toby snapped pulling his arm away. Lola pouted but followed Toby anyway.

Chapter 45

Diesel leaned into Miley's side as the elevator door closed. "Hey," he smiled softly.

"Hey," Miley sighed hanging her head, tears threatened to spill but she could not exactly say why.

"Hanging in there?" Diesel asked.

"I guess," Miley groaned. "I don't want to be here."

"Let me help," Diesel said grabbing hold of Miley's hand and turning her back to him before she could protest he began rubbing circles on the surface of her skin and then made his way up to her shoulders rubbing. "I promise everything's going to be okay," he said kissing Miley's shoulder from behind her.

Miley's body tensed and Diesel smiled into her skin, "don't tense up." His words were soft, as he smiled more when he felt Miley's body respond to him. It was such a relief that Miley was respondent even though she resisted so much.

As the elevator slowed, he whispered one last thing, "Follow my lead." Miley simply nodded her head. Diesel lopped an arm around her waist and tugged her toward the now open door. The floor was quiet but together they walked over toward the receptionist desk.

"Mrs. Tanner," the receptionist asked.

"Please don't call me that. It's Miley and after the divorce my name's going to change," she scowled.

"Oh really," the receptionist sneered. Of course, Toby had to meet at his office; people here knew him and respected the prick but not her obviously.

"Yes," Diesel said coolly. "You could change it now… if you wanted."

"Uhg," the woman rolled her eyes at Miley but looked up googly-eyed at Diesel. "Who are you handsome?"

"Miley's fiance. It's about time this …" Diesel began.

Miley tugged frantically on his arm and harshly whispered into Diesel's ear as he leaned down to her. "You can't say that!" she hissed. She wasn't quite mad more like nervous.

"It's okay, love. We shouldn't need to hide it." Diesel shrugged and smiled over to the receptionist. "It is about time this divorce is over with don't you think?"

The receptionist nodded frantically. "Of course, I have been telling Toby that for months," she crooned.

"Miley?" a voice asked from the elevator doorway causing Miley and Diesel to turn around, now ignoring the receptionist.

"Oh thank goodness." Miley sighed. "Diesel, this is my lawyer, Mr. Ibsen."

"Diesel McBride," Diesel smiled holding out a hand to the lawyer.

"George Ibsen," the lawyer smiled shaking Diesel's hand. "Well, are we ready Miley?"

"As I can ever be," Miley let out a breath and let Diesel lead her behind George.

Chapter 46

Diesel had to keep from laughing as Toby floundered before them. He was obviously not interested in the woman who he had brought with him and the divorce actually did not seem to be going his way. Even worse, Toby was glaring death at him and Diesel really did not care.

"I want the companies!" Toby shouted.

"Those were mine before I married you! I inherited them," Miley huffed.

"But you work for the Siegel group you have the money. You don't need the businesses," Toby floundered again.

"I don't care. I want my things, especially the things that were mine all along, Toby. We were only married for a few days!"

"A three weeks!" Toby complained.

'That's because you wouldn't leave my house and I had to file the paperwork!" Miley sneered.

"Can we work this out by letting Toby have the apartment?" Toby's lawyer offered.

"That's my home!" Miley cried out. "He already got my parents to get rid of my house! I got the apartment after we were separated! Where would I live?" Miley huffed out in annoyance.

"This is getting us nowhere," George, Miley's lawyer shook his head.

"Can I speak with Miley alone one moment?" Diesel asked.

Miley's head turned quickly and she stared wide-eyed at Diesel. "Of course, we'll give this a moment to cool off," George nodded.

"Come with me love," Diesel said holding out a hand to Miley.

Miley gripped Diesel's hand and stood. Together they walked out of the room. As soon as the door closed, Diesel turned Miley to face him, pressing her against the wall. "Now… this is what I want to propose here…" Diesel began as he ran a hand along the side of Miley's cheek.

Miley nodded ready to agree to anything that Diesel would say. "Give him the apartment."

"What?" Miley squeaked. "That's my home."

"I know love. But you won't need it for long if I get my way and then he'll sign and all this would be over. I promise I will never betray you." Miley gasped clamping her hand over her mouth in shock.

"Diesel…" Miley murmured.

"You don't have to say anything now," Diesel smiled slightly. "But… I would like you to just let the idiot have the apartment. Move with me. You can stay in the guest house… if you would like," Diesel begged.

Miley nodded simply. "Okay. I'll give him the apartment."

That was not the most desirable of answers to all of what Diesel had said but… it was a start.

Together they walked back into the conference room. Miley could not help but hold a slight smile on her lips as she huffed out the words she spoke, "I should have made you sign a pre-nuptial."

"But you did not babe," Toby chuckled before rolling his eyes. "I want the dog."

"Go ahead keep the damn dog," Miley replied. "He can have the apartment as long as he signs," Miley said.

"Wait… I don't want it," Toby back tracked.

"Huh?" Miley's eyebrows furrowed.

"Well, if you don't want the dog then I don't," Toby snorted.

"Mister Tanner is this all the meeting is about?" Toby's lawyer snapped out the question and seemed quite angry by it. "Did you even hear she was offering the apartment?" his lawyer asked.

"I get the apartment?" Toby asked with a smile.

"Yeah, if you'll just sign the papers," George, Miley's lawyer, smiled. "Now…"

"I don't want the apartment now," Toby blurt out.

"Mister Tanner, what are we doing here?" Toby's lawyer barked.

"Well… she wasn't supposed to bring him," Toby argued pointing a finger toward Diesel angrily.

"Oh really," Miley shook her head sighing. "This is so ridiculous."

"I know dear. But, eventually he will be out of our life and we can move on with ours. I promise we'll get married as soon as this is settled," Diesel said softly leaning over and offering Miley a soft kiss on the cheek and a comforting small hug. He smiled ignoring Miley's slightly stunned, but quickly covered up look.

"WHAT!" Toby screamed.

"Mister Tanner, please keep your voice down… your giving me a headache," his lawyer complained. "I think this meeting is over. Mister Tanner, please just sign the document. It is the best offer you are going to receive. Let this poor girl get on with her life."

Diesel and Miley, along with Miley's lawyer, looked over at Toby's lawyer in disbelief. They could not believe he was trying to push Toby into signing but were very happy about it either way.

Toby let out an annoyed roar of anger before slamming his hand on the table "give me the damn paper," he growled.

The lawyer passed the two copies with a small nod. "Thank you," Miley let out softly. She would finally be free of the annoying man and horrible pained memories.

Miley squealed as Diesel squeezed her butt, they were walking out of the meeting with Toby and the lawyers. Diesel could not help, but grind salt into the wound further for Toby.

"Hey," Miley slapped Diesel's arm playfully. They were playful as they made their way down the hall to the elevator. Toby, angrily following behind them.

"Come here," Diesel puffed as he reached out and caught Miley as she tried to squirm away from him. His hands collapsed around her stomach and pulled her close kissing her cheek.

"Uhg, would you two just get a room," Toby hissed.

"Love to. Thanks for the idea," Diesel chuckled. Swiftly he reaching down and scooped Miley up into his arms tucking her in close. "Let's go love… its playtime."

Chapter 47

As Diesel climbed into the car, Miley quickly wrapped her arms around him pulling him close. "I owe you," she beamed kissing his cheek. The slight gesture was overwhelming to him. The girl was overly excited and she willingly kissed him, which made him happy.

They had driven back to Miley's apartment to celebrate with take-out. Afterward, Diesel was planning to take her somewhere where he could tell her all about himself.

"Yeah, the divorce is finalized." Miley spoke over the phone to someone. Diesel had excused himself to the restroom and she had received the call taking it as an okay to speak out in the living room.

"You need me to come back, really? I don't know… I have someone…" Miley paused listening to the person on the other side of the phone line. "Oh… I'm so sorry to hear that but…" Miley let out a soft sob, "I can't…" Diesel frowned as he stood in at the far side of the room listening Miley grunted, "fine. I will be there just give me… Okay. I'll be on the first flight out." Miley clicked the phone shut.

"Where are we going?" Diesel questioned, his eyebrow raised curiously.

"We aren't," Miley whimpered. "I am going. I don't know when I'll be back but you've got to go." Tears began to stream down Miley's cheeks and Diesel rushed forward to comfort her.

"Miley, I'll go anywhere with you."

"You can't. I have to go on my own." Miley said firmly.

"Miley," Diesel plead.

"I have to go. Please lock the door when you leave." Tears streamed down Miley's cheeks as she rushed into the bedroom. Luckily, she had a spare suitcase since the new one was in a foreign country without her. She tucked in some more comfortable lounging outfits and clothing that would work great for doing some manual labor.

Her family needed her to come home, though she really did not want to, it wasn't quite a request.

Miley allowed Diesel to drive her to the airport but that was it. She refused to allow Diesel to follow her inside. Diesel sighed nodded his head and drove away. He drove the car around to the long term parking and filled out a form to keep the car parked there.

Stepping from the attendant's office, Diesel looked around quizzically. Where could she have gone? He quickly made his way to the terminal. Stepping inside, Diesel lifted his head and took in a deep breath. He could pick up the scents of coffee brewing, food cooking, perfumes, colognes, and sweat. The scent of the woman he chose as a mate was somewhere close to the scent of coffee and Diesel began to walk toward it.

Diesel smiled when he finally spotted the familiar brunette slipping gingerly at a cup of coffee. A small amount of tears slipped down her cheeks but she remained somewhat composed. Diesel sucked in a deep breath, holding his beast back from reaching out to comforting her. He looked around and spotted a location he could hide and still see Miley. He needed to wait to find out what plane she was taking and where she was going.

After twenty minute, Miley sniffled and wiped the tears away before dumping her cup in the trash. She gripped onto her luggage then walked off. Diesel ducked behind objects, pillars, and people watching as Miley came to a set of terminal seating.

She began to sit down when someone called out, "Flight 143 now boarding for first and business class." Miley shifted her bag and sighed. Instead of continuing toward the stewardess, she moved closer and stopped. Another few minutes passed and Miley walked forward to hand the woman a ticket and continued down the hall to flight 143.

Chapter 48

Diesel had hurried away after he watched Miley walk onto the flight 143. He stopped at a board and checked where the plane was going and then hurried away. He could not fly quite as fast as the plane, so he wanted to leave as soon as possible.

Outside the airport, finding a place to shift was actually quite difficult. There was only one spot, which Diesel figured might be big enough. On the other side of the road from the airport was a wooded area. He sprinted down the drive and across the road as if he was running from a forest fire, his speed increasing as he neared it. Any human who would pay enough attention, might notice the inhuman speed, but Diesel did not care.

Launching his body over the security fencing with ease, Diesel raced faster. As he hit the tree cover, Diesel stripped his clothing off quickly tucking his jeans, shirt, underwear, socks, and shoes into a backpack, which had been specially made to attach around his calf. It was made specifically for his dragon by the crafters on the island. It would expand as his creature's body shifted.

Fully naked and his clothing pack in place, Diesel closed his eyes and held out his arms calling for his dragon to rise to the surface. In a hurry now that Miley was getting further and further away, the dragon pushed harder rising quicker than Diesel had ever shifted before.

The more time a dragon spent with the mate they chose, the faster they could shift, especially an alpha. Within a matter of second, Diesel's skin began to wiggle and move while the bones beneath twisted, turned, and grew. His face elongated, his digits stretching into long toes and claws. His teeth grew sharp as needles and his skin began to turn into the pearly black scales of his dragon.

Now standing around fifteen foot tall and almost twice in length, Diesel knew his powers were going to be pushed to the limit as he flew for his first daylight flight. Humans would be completely ignorant to not spot the way the trees swayed and argued against the massive beast's body as he moved out into the open but they wouldn't be able to notice him. Diesel was more than lucky that he had the knowledge and strength to pull it off but turning such a massive creature invisible really was quite hard.

The delicate now invisible wings of the beast swooped down to the ground before flying back up; he was taking flight from the ground. Moving with the speed of a trained warrior, Diesel lifted himself up and flew toward the southwest.

Miley's plane had lifted off nearly a half an hour ago and had quite a lead on him. Yet, he had the determination to find her again. Diesel would follow her to the end of the earth to bring his mate back to his side.

Heavy whoops of his massive wings sounded like a freight train moving through the sky. The sound was so loud that humans walking around the airport lifted their heads to the sky searching for it. Diesel held in a chuckle as he flew over their heads. It would have been fun to play with the human by blowing fire into the sky or letting out a roar but he knew better.

Pushing his dragon to move fast Diesel's wings flapped furiously against the air. The plane would touch down in hours. Diesel on the other hand wouldn't land for a few after that. He would then have to located her scent and track her down. Would his mate be happy to see him again, he wasn't quite sure, but he was worried about it.

By the time Diesel landed, he was tired. He could not believe his mate flew from New York to Colorado on a what, a whim?

After he had landed near the airport, he had tracked down her scent. The lovely smell went in one direction, straight from the plane to what must have been a waiting car or taxi then headed north.

Once Diesel had shifted himself back into his dragon, he flew low trying desperately to keep even the slightest link on her scent. Luckily it was a nice day out and most of the cars had their windows open, the one Miley had rode in was not any different.

He landed himself near a small pond on the property of a large farm. The dragon was well hidden, he believed, so he took slow steps toward the water to quench his thirst before shifting.

He let loose his invisibility to relax some. Miley was close and he could feel her; there was no more need to rush. Lapping up the cool refreshing water, Diesel curled his long tail around his back legs then laid his head down over his front ones. He would rest here for a while letting his beast calm and rejuvenate in his true form.

A young girl's laughter caused Diesel to break out of his resting slumber. "Oh Willy, this is so pretty" the girl cooed. There were two of them, Diesel thought as he swiftly brushed his tail over the tracks he had left in the sand. His body was beginning to turn invisible when the girl spotted him. "Look!" she called out.

Her voice did not hold fear but more like curiosity as she crept closer. "I can't believe it. There's a giant lizard."

Diesel turned around. The girl was creeping closer and closer reaching out her hand to touch the spike along his tail. "Did not anyone tell you, it's impolite to touch...," Diesel hissed gently.

The girl screeched and jumped back pulling her hand away from Diesel's now semi open, sharp teethed mouth. "How can you talk?" The boy who must have been Willy asked.

"All of my kind can speak," he rolled his shoulders back and stood up proudly. "Do you know a Miley Tanner?" he asked. Since the children were out here bothering him and he would have to change their memories anyway, he figured he would ask.

"Aunt Miley?" the girl giggled. "Of course we know her," the girl's voice was soft and bubbly as she slowly tried again to reach Diesel's spiked tail.

"Would you like to feel my tail?" he chuckled.

"Yes, please," the girl nearly whispered.

"To bad," Diesel huffed swishing it away from her.

The girl's face paled and tears threatened to spill, but then Diesel did something he never thought he could do. Slowly, he brought his head down to the girl's level and allowed her to touch his silky smooth scales.

Her tiny little fingers laced around the horn on the end of his nose refusing to let go. "You have a horn like a hippo-pona-moose," she smiled.

"Rhinoceros?" Diesel provided tilting his head slightly.

"That's what she meant," the boy laughed. The little girl just scowled. "My name's Will. What do you want with my sister?" he asked. The boy was only young but he acted as if he was the stern older brother protecting his sister.

"I am a friend. Can you tell me how to find her?" the dragon asked tipping his head down and relaxing his wings to his sides as he swished his tail back and forth.

"She's up at the house with momma," the girl offered softly.

"Thank you," Diesel answered, still in dragon form. Then he nuzzled the little girl's side before speaking again, "Sleep, it's all a dream."

It would not make the children sick, nor would it make them get hurt. The two children slowly slipped to the ground falling asleep. Rapidly shifting into his human form, Diesel pulled on his clothing before checking in on the children once again. They would only be asleep for a few minutes and he made his way toward the house in the distance before they woke.

Diesel's sensitive hearing noticed the children beginning to wake. They then began to ask each other questions curiously. He smiled. Children's minds are so easily manipulated.

Chapter 49

The house was a farm house, yet it was so much bigger. It was large, beautiful, and white. The house sported a wraparound porch. Behind it, Diesel could recognize a barn and field. Fencing stretched out behind the house and barn where animals must have been pastured at.

He contemplated just walking up to the door and knocking or sneaking into the room, which Miley slept in at night… the sun was beginning to fade and so Diesel took the easier route. He strode straight up to the door and knocked.

After a few minutes there was shuffling on the other side of the door. He smiled politely as a woman with graying brown hair answered the door. Her eyes were brown and her skin tanned from the sun.

"Well hello," the woman smiled softly. She was young, if you took away the age lines and blond hair color she had she would look as if she was Miley's twin.

"Hello," Diesel said back. "Is Miley Tanner here?"

"Oh! Of course, who are you her boyfriend?" the woman gleamed. Her features seemed to light up some, as she looked Diesel up and down.

"Um yeah, something like that," Diesel grinned. "May I see her?"

"Sure. Let me get her. Take a seat," the woman said holding her arm out toward the chairs along the deck.

"Thanks," Diesel smiled sitting down.

He smirked to himself when he could hear the woman's voice talking adamantly to whom he figured must have been Miley on the other side of the wall. "What do you mean there's a man outside for me?" Miley asked.

"Oh come on Miley, how could you not tell me you had such a hottie boyfriend. He came all the way here to see you and you're not going to go outside and get him?" the girl complained.

"I don't have a boyfriend," Miley complained. "I just finished my divorce. Why would I want a boyfriend? After what Toby did… no way. I'll go tell him to go away," Miley snorted and stomped toward the door.

"Miley," the girl complained again. "It's late. Let him stay, if you don't want him…" the woman's voice paused "I'll be more than happy to let him sleep in my bed."

Diesel shook his head; he heard a grunt of disapproval before the door yanked open. Miley's head popped out and she looked around, her eyes settling on Diesel with a glare.

"I'll be outside Becca, you stay away from him." Miley pulled the door tightly behind her and stomped toward Diesel. His body shot up from the chair and caught her within his arms. For the moment, he forgot that Miley did not want him here.

"What are you doing here?" she growled.

"Miley, I can't be without you. Come back with me," Diesel begged.

"I don't want to talk about this right now. You need to leave," she hissed.

"Oh no he doesn't Miley; come on in handsome," Becca smiled holding the door open for him.

Diesel's saddened expression faded and he smiled down at Becca as he passed. "Thanks," he whispered softly.

"He's not going to be your new play toy," Miley groaned, "get over it."

"It's dinner time. Are you hungry, Mister?" Becca paused.

"Rebecca, this is Diesel. Now will you please leave him alone," Miley begged.

"Miley, why don't you ring the bell? It's nice to meet you Diesel," Becca beamed. "Why don't you come sit by me?"

Miley grunted in complaint but did as her sister asked. If not, she was sure to hear a mouthful from her mother. How could Becca be trying to hit on Diesel right in front of her? Though it seemed like Diesel was ignorant, she knew he could tell what Becca was up to, but he did not let it faze him.

"I think I'll sit with Miley, but thank you."

Chapter 50

It had only been moments before thundering footfalls erupted around the house. Not long before the house filled with voices as everyone focused their attention on Diesel. Miley had made her way to the cupboards pulling out plates and setting them on the counter. "Do you mind if I help?" Diesel asked coming up behind her.

"Sure," Miley surrendered.

"And who might you be?" a woman's annoyed voice asked.

"This is Diesel, mother," Becca cooed. "He came to see Miley," she dragged out the words and Diesel could instantly feel the annoyance and jealousy radiating off Becca.

"Get ready for all hell to break loose," Miley whispered from the side of Diesel.

"What?" Miley's mother's face scrunched into confusion before she screamed, "ROGER!"

Diesel tried his best not to flinch to cover his ears as multiple people came into the room and looked at the woman in confusion.

"Miley, who is he!"

"I am her fiance," Diesel butted in before Miley could speak.

That was the moment when all ciaos broke. Some people burst out laughing while others gasped in shock and Miley curled herself into Diesel's side trying to become invisible.

"Good man!" someone barked in laughter, while another shrieked 'how could you.'

Miley's mother grit her teeth, sucked in a sharp angry breath, and pointed toward the doorway. "Miley," she said very slowly, "please bring your friend into the sitting room. We need to have a family talk."

"I…" Diesel began to protest, but Miley found her words.

"No," she blurt out. "He stays, right here."

"Well-I-aught-a," Miley's mother gasped.

"Mother, he's staying for a while," Miley shrugged and sat down at the table.

There was stunned silence for a few moments while everyone watched Miley's mother stew in anger. Soon a man entered the room and everyone began to pick at the utensils near their plates or chat amongst themselves quietly.

"Well hello," the man smiled. "I am Roger. Who must you be?" he said walking up to Diesel with an out stretched hand.

"Diesel McBride," Diesel smiled genuinely, "Miley's fiance."

"Ha," Roger laughed. "Good man," he chuckled while patting Diesel on the shoulder. "I thought she would never settle down…" He then turned his gaze toward Miley's mother, "Well Samantha, what do ya think about that? I thought you invited Winston to the gathering just so you could get him and Miley together."

Roger was smiling, but nearly everyone stared without words, watching how Samantha would react to everything. "I can't believe this!" Miley screamed. "Another man mother really!"

"Well, someone has to find you the right man. Your grandfather would be rolling in his grave if he saw you now," Samantha screeched before stomping away.

Roger smiled. "Well everyone, let's eat. I'm sure she'll come back when she's hungry," Roger chuckled.

Diesel hugged Miley beside him. He loved the simplicity of touching her skin. She needed comforting and he wasn't going to let the moment be passed up.

"So Mister McBride, why don't you tell us about yourself?" Roger asked as he scooped the first scoops of food onto his plate.

Chapter 51

Diesel had been more than happy to speak with Miley's father. The man had been very welcoming and enjoyable, yet he could sense the uneasiness that came from everyone as soon as Miley's mother returned. Roger asked no more questions and everyone seemed to quiet down.

One child decided it was time to break the ice, and spoke up. "You're familiar," she said looking up at him with curiosity. Diesel smiled down at her. The girl was young, probably around six years old. She was the very same girl, which he had talked to in the trees.

"Well what is your name beautiful?" He asked.

"Sami," the girl beamed. "I am eight."

"Wow. I would never have guessed." Diesel chuckled, "would you like some more meat lovely?"

"Yes please," the girl squared her shoulders and proudly pronounced.

Diesel nodded and reached for the chicken tongs, his hand hovered over the meat as the girl spoke again. "That's Moose. Momma said it was time to eat her so… we had to cook her. Chickens can't be eaten unless their cooked."

Diesel's face paled, as he turned back to the little girl horrified.

"Just ignore it," Miley giggled from beside him. "Sami please stop grossing out the guest, go sit at the children's table," Miley scolded softly.

Sami frowned, stood up, and took her plate from Diesel before walking away from the table. Diesel relaxed back into the chair some as the girl left. How could a little child, be so blunt, he wondered. Thank goodness Miley was there to relieve him from the situation because he wasn't sure what he would have said if he had to stand there and chat with the little blond girl who he had thought would have been so completely innocent.

The remainder of dinner went well. Diesel answered the questions that Miley's family asked with skilled ease. It was a regularly practiced thing for the men on his island whom traveled to prepare for questions.

"Miley you should tell your friend he needs to leave, you don't even know him. He cannot go to the get together tomorrow." Miley's mother, Samantha glared. "I am going to have to say no on your inheritance and cut you out of the will as well if you don't send him away."

"Oh Samantha, just hush up woman. This is a wonderful man." Roger winked in Miley's direction.

"Look at him, Roger," she hissed. "He's not anything like us, he's so beneath her. What will the party guests think?"

"Isn't it bad enough that you had to lie to your daughter to get her here?" Roger snorted.

Diesel sighed. He now understood a little why Miley had been so upset and left in a rush. "Yes. I do hear what you are saying Samantha, I am definitely not much like you. I am much stronger than the tiny man, which Miley was pretty much forced into marrying before. I would never put a woman down, or treat her the way that Toby treated her. I would most certainly never sleep around if I had a woman, especially, one as perfect as Miley. And I am definitely not after her for money."

"Yeah, I'm so gone to believe a man who looks like he went shopping at a thrift store and forgot to wash after working in the fields," Samantha huffed.

Diesel snorted and looked down at himself. "I may not be dressed to please you and I may be in quite a need of a bath since I have been in a hurry lately, but I most certainly can tell you I am not who you think I am."

Samantha was about to respond when Miley let out a frustrated breath and shoved her chair backward as she stood up. "That's enough for tonight. I believe we will be retiring for the night," she grabbed hold of Diesel's arm and yanked him up with her.

"Diesel is going to share a room with you right?" Becca asked coming around a corner.

"Becca," Miley snorted. "Don't push it."

"Miley. He's hot. I'm just saying if you're not interested …" Miley cut Becca's ranting off with a finger to her lips.

"Listen. He'll have a place to sleep don't worry," Miley scowled walking away.

Becca rolled her eyes and continued on her way. Miley snatched up Diesel's hand and dragged him down the hall and up the long stairway to the upstairs. Once safely inside the room she would be sleeping in, Miley closed the door and let out a soft breath.

"So… are you staying the night?" Miley asked softly.

"Yes," Diesel smirked as he approached her slowly. "I shall and I am going to be staying with you."

"You won't be spending the night in my bed," Miley rolled her eyes.

Diesel gripped her hips and Miley let out a small screech. "Love… I'll stay where ever you stay even if I need to take the floor."

"But…" Miley muttered.

"Love, you won't and neither will I be able to sleep without each other near. Tomorrow, we'll take a walk and we will make sure you remember every bit of the island clearly. I will also explain everything that you did not learn," Diesel said.

"That would be nice," Miley sighed, "Because you're really starting to grow on me," she muttered under her breath.

Miley was having the hardest time with everything. She desperately wanted to be in Diesel's strong arms, yet she was nervous about her past experiences. Then when it came to her family, well everything was a mess.

"I am going to take a shower…" Miley said softly.

Diesel smirked, "Mind if I join?"

Miley's eyes widened and her mouth hung as she floundered with the words to say.

His smirk grew into a full-blown smile. Stepping closer to Miley with a devilish glint in his eye, he promised her everything without saying anything. He gently lifted Miley up until her feet did not touch the floor any longer.

Her arms flew up around his neck and her legs around his hips. Diesel pushed Miley against the wall and pressed his lips down upon hers. Moments later, only pulling away slightly, his words ragged and husky he said, "I am going to pleasure you…"

Chapter 52

Though Miley and Diesel had a passionate time in the shower, when they returned to the bedroom, everything was once again tense. He could sense Miley's rising anxiety and he regretted not letting himself get carried away.

"I will not make love to you until you're ready," he told her. "We have still things to discuss before we do that."

"Like what?" Miley asked him curiously, as her hands ran up and down his naked water soaked body. He was so stunning that she could not help but want him.

"Just let me pleasure you tonight and tomorrow may be different." He promised as he pushed her back against the shower wall.

Miley's body had been so responsive to his loving touches. Wrapping an around Miley's tiny thigh while the other he traced up and down Miley stomach Diesel gently had traced his tongue along her body.

He had held back his dragon with the strongest of mental chains he could use. He could feel the pressure getting to him, but he wouldn't make love to her until she knew everything.

"I guess you may take the bed since you're the guest." Miley frowned. "I'll take the chair."

Diesel raised an eyebrow at Miley then looked to the chair. "Love?" He questioned.

"Don't worry," Miley groaned as she pulled her legs up into her lap trying to get comfortable.

Miley had twisted and turned for what seemed like way too long and Diesel could not take it anymore. Shoving the covers back from the bed, he pushed himself up, and patted over to the chair where Miley had attempted to sleep.

"That's enough," Diesel said softly as he tucked his arms around her back and under her thighs.

"Diesel," Miley whined tiredly.

"Why can't we just lay in the same bed? I want you by my side. I want to get some sleep, just as much as I know you need to," he argued. Diesel was sure that their time in the shower had made Miley feel wanted yet he could also tell that is what made her shy away. Setting her down in the bed and covering her up, he walked around to the other side of the bed and climbing beneath the covers.

"I know you won't," Miley mumbled softly as she curled herself into the covers and closed her eyes, falling asleep almost instantly with the delicious scent of Diesel on the pillows.

Chapter 53

"Did you enjoy yourself last night?" Diesel's smirking face looked down at Miley, who was curled into his chest trying desperately to stay sleeping.

"Shh… sleeping," she yawned.

"And you're so not interested in me…" Diesel chuckled.

"Isn't that obvious from last night?" Miley questioned. She was all over him, she remembered, but he had only let himself touch her without letting her pleasure him. It had frustrated her.

"Soon," Diesel whispered gently wrapping an arm around her.

Miley sighed, "Fine, now will you please let me go."

"Will you stay?" Diesel asked. He was stuck between being a jerk that followed her around and being a sweet loving man. Miley was not quite sure, which he was, but she did not know for sure if she really wanted to find out.

Miley squirmed trying to get out of Diesel's grip, "I promise my love, I am nothing like the low life you were married too." He leaned down and gently kissed Miley's lips.

"Did you not hear my mother last night?"

"I did and I clearly heard you as well." Diesel also did not mention he had heard every bit even the bits that Miley's human ears could not hear when they walked away.

"Samantha, I like him." Roger had said.

"But Roggie, what if he's only after her for our money," Samantha's voice was whiny and Diesel could hear the discomfort within it.

"Someday, you will have to let Miley grow on her own. She's not like Rebecca. She's an independent woman and Rebecca well…" there was a pause before Roger began again. "Though we are bringing the guests over to our home tomorrow for the party, I think you should tell Miley, you're sorry for everything. I will ask Diesel if he's interested in going shopping for something new for the reunion. I think you girls need some time."

"Roger," Samantha's voice was stern and hurt sounding. "I am not sorry. I do not want her to marry him. I want her to marry Toby or Winston or maybe even Patrick. Roger… she took the man to her bed."

"I've had enough. Miley's a grown woman, who I am sure has had her share of fun time. I don't care if you feel it's necessary for Miley to marry who you like or not. I'm not losing my daughter over your petty difference in opinion. So you will tell her you're sorry for everything, beginning with the hurtful words you said to her over the phone."

That had been the last of the conversation before two had settled down for the night.

"Why don't you take a shower…?" Miley said, breaking Diesel from his thoughts.

Diesel was pleased with this. He quickly sat up and pushed from the bed. Miley was left to stare at his half-naked torso. She blushed and quickly turned her head away.

"Stare all you like love… but remember I will stare too," he smirked. The scent of Miley's desire was such a sweet smell which had spiked almost instantly. He liked the effect he had on her. "Remember, we will be going for a walk later so we can… talk."

Diesel then turned and walked across the room leaving Miley dumbfounded. She had forgotten about Diesel's 'talk' and was hoping he had as well ,but nope. It seemed as if she wouldn't get away from him that easily.

"Want to come with me?" he asked shocking Miley.

"Uh… no thank you, maybe another time" Miley muttered.

Diesel smiled "I'll remember that."

Miley let out a breath of relief as Diesel disappeared into the bathroom. Quickly, she scurried across the bedroom and pulled on new undergarments. As she was about to pull on a dress, Diesel poked his head back out of the bathroom.

"Love, I'll be down in a minute. Oh, by the way… I like …" Miley gasped and yanked her dress down over her.

"I'll be downstairs," she was out the door and down the hall in a flash.

Chapter 54

Miley looked around, the house was semi quiet, different from the day before. "Oh, hi dad," Miley said as she spotted her father in the kitchen reading the newspaper.

"Morning darling," Roger smiled. "Where is Diesel, I wanted to talk with him."

"Oh, uh…" Miley blushed as she looked back toward where she had walked from, "he's taking a shower."

"Well when he's finished, I want to chat with him," Roger told her. "Oh, dear, your mother's expecting you back at the house. She was hoping you could help direct the event coordinators around."

"Oh okay. I guess I'll go and tell Diesel a moment…" Miley murmured.

"Tell me what love?" Diesel purred as he wrapped his arm around Miley's shoulder and pulled her closer to him. She blushed.

"She was just going to say, that I wanted to have a chat with you and Miley's mother is expecting her back at our home." Roger said casually. "Get a move on dear; you don't want to make your mother wonder where you are."

Miley looked at Diesel, searching his eyes for any sign that he was nervous about the chat with her father, but she could see nothing. There was no sign of fear in his eyes, no nervousness, and no worry. He leaned down and kissed Miley gently on the cheek, "Don't want to keep her waiting. I'll see you in a little while."

Miley nodded and Diesel turned her around in his arms, tapping her on the butt to hurry her along. She squeaked which made both men chuckle.

"So, what is it you wanted to speak to me about?" Diesel asked.

"I was wondering if you would allow me to take you out to get you something nice to wear to the party." Roger smiled.

Diesel eyed the man curiously. Roger sat with his legs crossed, the newspaper he was reading was flopped over, and he was wearing a pristine black Armani suit. The man looked as if he was made of money as simple as that. Diesel cocked an eyebrow and was about to question when Roger spoke up quickly, "I mean no disrespect, I swear. I only mean to make peace. You did come here without luggage am I correct."

Diesel nodded "You are very correct, sir."

"So shall we?" Roger asked.

Shrugging Diesel nodded slightly, "Why not."

"Great!" Roger beamed as he stood up and walked toward the door, "let's go."

Diesel followed instep casually behind Roger. As they walked out behind the house, Diesel noticed for the first time a black Corvette convertible. "Nice car," Diesel grinned.

"Oh, you like it?" Roger asked as he climbed inside and began to put the top down. "My wife doesn't think it's good enough for me," Roger scoffed, "but I love it."

"Women," Diesel laughed.

"I know!" Roger chuckled.

The two men enjoyed the ride talking about the things they could never understand about women. "I never understood how women can go from happy to crying in moments," Roger muttered.

"I may not have been around as long as you have sir," Diesel said slowly, "but I gave up on understanding a woman's mind years ago."

Roger laughed. "Well it looks like we're here my boy." He parked the car and stepped out still laughing as they both walked toward the building.

Chapter 55

"Hello Miley," Samantha muttered.

"Mother," Miley replied. "What needs to be done?"

"Listen Miley," Samantha said stepping closer to Miley. She held her hand out and reached to pat her daughter on the arm.

"Mother!" Becca called out. She had just walked in the door and abruptly interrupted, stomping on Samantha's courage instantly.

"Oh Rebecca darling," Samantha said stepping around Miley, "I'm in here dear!"

Miley sighed looking back toward the couch as she slumped down. Her pink and white dress poofed up on its way to settle down. Samantha turned back around "Miley that is not very appropriate," She scoffed. "Why don't you go help the staff in the kitchen."

Miley muttered under her breath but did not bother to say much out loud. Rebecca had always been the favorite. Samantha and Rebecca laughed to themselves as Miley continued out of the room.

"Morning everyone!" Miley called as she walked in the large kitchen.

All of the staff looked up greeting her with bright smiles "your mother…" one woman scoffed pulling out a chair for Miley at the far side of the kitchen "doesn't she realize you're dressed up for the party."

"It's alright June," Miley groaned as she sat down. She pulled her chair up to the edge of the counter before grabbing a knife and a potato.

"You don' have to do that," another one of the staff complained.

"Oh hush," Miley shrugged. "It'll get done faster if I help."

"What if your mother comes in here?" June said. June was the older woman, which Miley had helped in the kitchen a lot during her years.

Smiling with a bit of an evil glint in her eyes Miley said, "You know better than that woman. My mother wouldn't be caught dead…"

"Your mother wouldn't be caught dead what?" Roger chuckled as he walked in followed by Diesel.

Miley blushed. "Don't leave me hanging Miley," Roger laughed as he walked toward her and grabbed a potato.

"Oh no you don't," the old woman scolded yanking the potato from Roger's hands, "not you too. It is hard enough keeping Miley here from getting in trouble with Miss Samantha. I don't need a scolding from her about you getting that suit dirty."

Roger shrugged. "Why don't we head in the other room and watch a movie why Diesel gets dressed."

That was the first time Miley had noticed the long suit bag draped over Diesel's arm. He smiled down at her. "I hope you'll like it."

"I'm sure you'll look as handsome as ever," Miley said quietly.

Roger slapped Diesel on the shoulder, "I told you."

"Told him what?" Miley asked as Roger began to walk away. "Hey! What did you tell him, Dad!"

Diesel laughed grabbing Miley's hand and tugging her after her father. "Come on love, you'll be alright."

When Roger finally came to a stop, he turned back toward them. "This is a guest room, you can change in here. We'll be right down the hall at the end."

"Very well," Diesel nodded. Roger walked away and before Miley could protest, Diesel pushed the door open and pulled Miley inside.

Quickly he turned around and pressed her up against the wall. "I've missed you." Diesel purred as he pressed his lips to her.

Instantly Miley's arms snapped up on their own accord and around his neck gripping him tightly. She moaned. Diesel's hands rubbed her bare legs and slowly roamed up beneath her dress.

She could no longer resist how much she wanted him. Diesel was a good man and she knew he would never hurt her. Miley wanted him at that moment more than she has ever wanted a man. She did not want him to let her go.

Suddenly, as quickly as he had pushed her against the wall he pulled back leaving her breathless. "Did I do something wrong?" she breathed.

Diesel smiled. "No love."

Dropping to his knee, Diesel pulled out a small box from his pocket. "I wanted to do this the right way. I already got your father's permission and now I'm going to ask you," he looked up at her grinning ear-to-ear as he continued.

"Miley, ever since the first day I met you, I knew I was doomed to love you. Your smile could warm the heart of the coldest heart and your laughter is as light and beautiful as that of angels. I love you and I will never ever hurt you like the unmentionable man did to you. Would you do me the honor of marring me?" he asked, grasping Miley's hand he slid an amazing white gold diamond solitaire ring onto her finger.

Chapter 56

Miley could barely breathe let alone speak as she walked on weak wobbly legs toward the media room. Roger turned to look at her from his recliner chair smiling. "So, you took quite some time."

"Yeah," Miley said letting out a breath.

She had left the room so Diesel could change. Slumping onto the couch beside her father, she stared down at her hand. "I thought that was the perfect one for you," Roger said quietly.

"You helped him chose?" Miley asked.

"Well not really, I just confirmed Diesel's thoughts. It's a very stunning ring. I'm sure your mother's going to have a heart-attack and your sister!" Roger laughed. "Oh well we'll just let her find out for herself, I think it's going to be one heck of a dinner party!"

Miley smiled.

"She said YES!" Diesel boomed as he walked into the room. He walked up to Miley bending down and pulled Miley to a standing position before sitting down and tugging her onto his lap.

"I knew she would," Roger shrugged.

"Dad?" Miley questioned. How could he of known she would say yes? Miley was still catching up with reality.

"Oh don't dad, me. Miley you should have seen the look on your face. You could barely keep yourself from touching the man all dinner last night. I know how you are darling, and I know whether you were about to admit it or not, he stole your heart."

Miley shook her head with a slight smile and laid her head down against Diesel's chest simply listening to his heart beat as they waited for the dinner guests to arrive.

Chapter 57

It had been a whole movie and a half since they had settled down in the media center then doorbell rang. "I'll get it," Miley said standing up. "The staff are all busy, I'm sure," she continued as she made her way out and down the hall.

Miley popped her head into the kitchen as she passed calling "I've got it," just so the staff would not get more overwhelmed.

As she passed the living room, she spotted her mother and Becca still chatting and laughing, completely uncaring that there was someone at the door. She scoffed.

When Miley finally reached the door, she yanked it open smiling "Welcome," then gasped at whom she saw.

"Hello to you too," Orion replied.

"How did you find me?" Miley grunted.

"Diesel's here," Orion shrugged.

"And…" Miley dragged out.

Orion chuckled darkly, "you've got so much to learn."

Miley frowned, "What's that supposed to mean?"

"We're linked. Diesel and I…" Orion shrugged as Miley's face scrunched up in confusion. "It's a difficult and confusing process. I'm sure he'll link with you once you're married. I'm sure he wouldn't want to lose you again," Orion smiled then added. "Can I come in?"

"Ah… yeah," Miley said stepping back and allowing Orion inside. Other guests had begun to arrive in the driveway and Miley grunted. "Do you mind stopping by the kitchen on our way…"

"Of course not," Orion shrugged.

Miley lead the way, stopping at the kitchen to alert the staff of the other pending guests to arrive at the door, then continued on to the media room. "Orion," Diesel smiled standing up. He stepped forward and held out his hand to sake with Orion.

Miley watched in curiosity as the two men stayed with linked hands for longer than she would have assumed. When they pulled apart they both seemed different… more relaxed with a slightly 'brighter' complexion.

That was strange; she thought, and immediately noted to ask about it later. "Roger this is my brother, Orion," Diesel smiled. "I hope you don't mind, I had invited him to celebrate with us," he said looking over at Miley; she knew he did not want her to protest.

"Of course not!" Roger beamed. "This is going to be entertaining."

Chapter 58

The dinner now was in full swing. Guests had arrive, nearly one hundred of them. They were mostly business associates, but a few 'friends of the family' lingered around as well.

Miley now knew exactly why her mother had demanded she come back home by lying through her teeth; they had to keep up appearances. Samantha was too proud to say 'my daughter left for New York because she did not want to be married to Toby.' Instead, she had invited Toby and hoped Miley would come alone and 'make appearances.'

With a loud whistle and a clinking of glass, Roger stood. "What are you doing?" Samantha hissed.

Roger ignored his dramatic wife and began to speak. "Friends and colleagues, may I have your attention please. I have some wonderful news to tell you all!"

"Oh my god!" Miley moaned, ducking her head as she blushed fiercely. Diesel chuckled and gripped Miley's hand giving her a bit of comfort.

"I hope you all have enjoyed the delicious dinner that was prepared by our wonderful staff and catering service." Everyone around the room clapped.

"As we are coming to a close tonight," Roger continued. "I would like to extend open arms to the guests that have had way too much to drink and a driver for those too proud to admit they drank too much," laughter erupted, Roger smiled but continued.

"As you all have noticed…" Roger's eyes flit over toward Miley and Diesel then back to the crowd, "I know most of you have spoken with Diesel. Please stand, Diesel, Miley you too darling." Roger waved his hand toward them smiling like crazy.

Miley stood slowly, her legs were wobbly and she was extremely thankful that Diesel wrapped a supportive arm around her waist. "I would like to formally introduce the engagement of my daughter Miley to this great man, Diesel."

The room erupted in clapping and cheering, followed by screeching from Rebecca and Samantha. Both woman huffed angrily as they pushed from the table. "Thank you all for coming. I'm sorry for my wife's abrupt departure, but I hope you all can understand. Goodnight and I'll be looking forward to hearing from you at a later date," Roger beamed.

He turned toward Miley and Diesel, "I'm sorry darling, if you would like to come with, you may, but I really need to go after your mother. We should really have a family meeting as soon as the guests are gone."

Miley nodded but stayed in her place. "I'll make sure everyone gets out safely," she promised.

"I wouldn't expect anything more," Roger nodded walking away.

Miley, Diesel, and Orion helped the guests get everything settled and even helped a few of the staff stack the dishes onto the trolley. As the last guest of the guests were leaving, Samantha's loud, angry voice could be heard, making Diesel snap his head in that direction.

"Go ahead. I'll make sure everything's handled," Orion assured them as he continued to help people.

"Samantha you're being unreasonable!" Roger nearly screamed.

"Roger, I am not being unreasonable. What could that man possibly come from? I have never heard of his family name. He's poor."

Diesel's furry was boiling now. What did money have to do with love? He gripped tightly to Miley's hand accidently making her whimper, before he let off some of his pressure. "Sorry," he muttered.

"Samantha, he's a good man. I spent a while with him and he's very kind," Roger said less harshly than before.

"Roger, I don't care if he's kind. How is he going to be able to care for her if he's poor," Samantha screamed.

Diesel let go of Miley's hand. Anger reached the max and Diesel roared as he burst into the room. He was going to show Samantha exactly whom she was dealing with.

"Who do you think you are?" he growled.

"Who am I? Who are you to be talking to me like that? I am Samantha Tanner, the wife of the mayor of Blue Harbor and…" Diesel cut her off holding up his hand to stop her from speaking.

"Yes ma'am, I have heard all about your husband's job, from him actually. And yes, I have heard you are from one of the wealthiest families in the state, of course, from your husband as well. But frankly, I really don't give a flying rat's ass." His words were blunt and caused Samantha to gasp as she held her hand to her heart.

"Roger! See what I mean!" Samantha whined. "He's so uncivil!"

"Enough!" Diesel growled annoyed, his anger was in check, but just by the slightest of strings. He was shaking with rage at the moment, "I am going to marry your daughter. I don't quite care if you are in her life or not after we leave this awful place. And truthfully, I have way more money to support anything Miley may ever want or need, therefore, no I'm not after her inheritance and I don't care if she ever sees a dime."

Diesel huffed. Miley stepped up beside him, gripping his shaking shoulder firmly. "I extend an open invitation, for any of the family that Miley may choose to invite, to come to our wedding via my personal jet," he was more than happy to invite them on the jet, even though he had never actually used it, more of a show piece than anything. "But I am going to tell you right now… if you dare open your mouth to complain or make Miley upset, one more time…" Diesel grunted, looked over at Miley then back to Samantha before continuing, "then that invitation to visit, will be cancelled and never renewed."

With that, Diesel turned on his heels clutching Miley's hand and towing her along behind him. Stopping for a moment, he let out his last words, "Thank you Roger for the pleasant time, but WE are leaving; if Miley so chooses then she will send an invention when the time comes."

Chapter 59

"That was incredible!" Miley murmured excitedly as she packed up her bag.

"Uh darling, I can tell you right now that he's not going to make it to the tree-line if you don't move along!" Orion grunted nodding his head toward an infuriated Diesel.

"Oh!" Miley said quickly, she had stopped packing up her things and walked slowly over toward Diesel. "You alright D's?"

"NO!" he hissed heatedly, his eyes were distant, but Diesel's arms reached out and caught Miley in them before she could move, pulling her in to comfort himself.

"Diesel, I can help her finish packing; why don't you go wait in the tree line?" Orion offered.

"And leave her here with an unmated Dragon!" Diesel snapped kissing her full on the mouth claiming his territory even if it was temporarily as he glared at his brother.

"I understand your concern, but even with this house as big as it is, I find it hard to believe that we can just walk out of here with a massive black dragon on our heels," Orion countered.

Diesel shook even more violently as he tried not to burst into his beast and kill Orion for the thought. "Miley," Orion said slowly holding a hand out to her.

She looked up at Diesel cautiously, and then turned slowly to face Orion. "There's only a few ways to calm him down and obviously the easiest one isn't working, he needs you right now or he'll be stuck in his dragon's form until we get back home," Orion told her.

"What do I need to do?" Miley said worriedly as she starred between the men.

Diesel was not himself. He held wild violet eyes that were enraged. He shook with anger.

"He's more beast now than human. There is only one option left. You must complete the bond. It will calm him. You can help him control his anger then," Orion begged.

"What!" Miley anxiously tried to pull out of Diesel's ever tightening grip. "He told me he wouldn't allow me to mate him until he explained everything!" she cried out.

"I'm sorry, but there's no other way," Orion sighed. "I'll let you two have some alone time. I'll be in my guest room when you are ready to go."

Miley looked up at Diesel's ever darkening eyes, trying to catch sight of any humanity left within them. Finally managing to wiggle her way free, she slowly made her way across the room. Diesel's eyes flit across the room and watched her every movement like a cat waiting to pounce.

She slowly cleared off the bed, zipping the last of the bags and dragging it over toward the door. Something in what she was wearing, the short upper-thigh length dress, that was laced around her neck and flowed around her freely, must have turned him on or at least flipped the switch in Diesel's head.

Within the blink of an eye, he was before her. Diesel wrapped one arm around Miley's tiny waist while the other slid up her bare thigh yanking at her underwear until they dropped to the floor. His movements were fluid, yet animalistic as he kissed from her lips down her throat and along any of the available skin.

Together, Miley and Diesel dropped onto the bed. She struggled to push him onto his back as so she could help him undress, but eventually settled with holding still while he did the job himself.

Once finally undressed he purred in satisfaction as he climbed back over her lifting the dress up over her head and tossing it across the room as he bent forward to kiss her bare skin once again.

Chapter 60

Orion could not stop smirking as he tried desperately to hold back his laughter. "Just say it and be done," Diesel grunted.

Miley groaned.

Orion burst out a breath and laughed. "That mark is by far the most girly one I have ever seen on such a dominant beast let alone an alpha!"

"I've seen it," Diesel rolled his eyes. "Actually we both did," he grinned toward his new mate.

Miley blushed as she reached a hand up slowly to rub the still slightly sore part of her throat. Diesel had apologized for many things including the part about not getting to take the walk they had planned for Diesel to explain everything. He also had told her the mark she now sported, was a part of the talk that would have happened.

Diesel moaned as his gaze shot over toward Miley. "Don't do that love," he purred.

"Huh?" Miley repeated. The new mark had a pleasurable euphoria for the person it was on, but it was mild. On the other hand, Diesel had to fight off the raging hormones to claim his mate again. "Oh!" Miley giggled softly before adding "sorry."

"But I've never seen anything like that! How did you even get out of the house without them noticing?" Orion laughed once again pointing at Diesel. He quickly regretted his decision though when Diesel's fist shot out and punched him square in the face.

Diesel grinned to himself. It gave him at least a bit of pleasure shutting Orion up. He thought back to the bedroom and when the mark had begun to etch it's way onto his beautiful mate's skin.

He had still been making love to her. Still inside of her when she began to whimper and grabbed for it. He watched with astonishment as the black mark formed along her delicate neck.

"I think it's interesting." Miley shrugged, though she did tug a shawl up around her shoulders trying to cover the mark as Orion lead the way through the house.

"Miley! Wait!" June called as she tried to hurry down the hallway. Diesel turned back around toward the sound of the woman; his face contorted showing his sympathy for the older woman.

Miley spun around, tears welling in her eyes as she ran toward the woman yanking herself free from Diesel's grasp. He growled protectively as he quickly grabbed Miley and tugging her to his chest.

Miley whimpered and looked up at Diesel. "She's like a mother to me," Miley cried softly.

Diesel let out a breath, flaring his nostrils and holding his lips into a thin tight line but he released his grip. "Go on," he said softly. How could he deny his mate a woman whom was like a mother to her?

Miley scurried from Diesel's grip and ran the remainder of the way into the June's waiting arms. "Shhh…" June soothed.

"I've missed you so much!" Miley whined.

"I know dear. It's been hard on all of us but me especially," June said softly.

"What if they never let me come back?" Miley cried. She hadn't been referring to Diesel and Orion. No, she was referring to the 'mother' that did not care for her.

"I'm sure I'll see you again someday soon. Did not I hear your fiance right, he offered for family to visit?" June said looking over toward Diesel.

He nodded, "I did and if it's alright with my future wife," Diesel paused for a moment eyeing Miley for any sign that she wouldn't be alright with what he was about to say. "I would love for Miley to have someone as close as a motherly figure with her at our home. I would like to ask if you would be willing to come and work for us?"

Miley squealed happily as she began bouncing on her heels impatiently. "I don't know…" June said slowly. "It's warm here. And I've worked here for years."

"June," Diesel chuckled. "How warm is it today at home Orion?"

"I believe it was…" Orion smirked looking over at the two women, "quite a hot day. What ninty-one?"

Diesel nodded, "That sounds about right."

"I guess it wouldn't hurt to come and visit for a little while and decide if I can handle the duties…" June grinned.

"That would be amazing!" Miley cried out excited.

Chapter 61

It had been a month since Miley and Diesel had returned to the island. A whole two months since they had settled everything at Miley's apartment. They had boxed up everything Miley was going to keep and donated everything, which she wasn't.

Orion had gone back to Morgan after determining that Diesel had made it home safely. He had already asked Diesel's permission to bring Morgan back to the island as his mate.

"Come on Diesel!" Miley moaned in annoyance. "Her boat's going to be here in two hours!"

"Miley!" Diesel snorted.

He was getting annoyed. He had promised to bring Miley up to the coast to greet June as she got off the boat but this was getting out of hand. "If you don't settle down and let me finish my work…" Diesel warned.

"What?" Miley complained. "What are you going to do to me big bad alpha dragon?" She taunted as she smacked playfully on Diesel's desk.

Growling Diesel pushed his chair back angrily. "She'll be here in two stinking hours! Will you please just go find something to do quietly in the other room?" His words were slow and calculated as he tried his best not to yell at his mate.

"Diesel!" Miley groaned. For some reason she just had to push his buttons lately. She smacked his desk accidently sending papers flying across the desk and landing on the floor at Diesel's feet.

Diesel pushed his chair back with so much force it slammed against the wall. Miley squealed as she turned around and ran. Bad idea, Diesel thought as he began to lose control.

By the time he had reached the back door, where Miley had run off too, he was holding on by a thread. In that moment Diesel had stepped foot onto the sandy back yard Miley had disappeared out of sight in the jungle surrounding, causing his playful yet annoyed dragon burst out and take over.

The black dragon roared as he pushed himself up into the air. He could easily hear his mates frantic heart beat as she raced across the island.

With only a few flaps of the massive dragon wings Diesel was upon his mate. Diesel dove down into the tree line shifting as he landed and wrapping his arms around Miley then twirling the both of them around so that he hit the ground beneath her.

"Why are you annoying me?" He hissed playfully as he held her hips tightly against his body.

"I…" Miley muttered anxiously. She had known by now that Diesel would not ever hurt her. She was just growing slightly anxious over the last few days and she could not quite explain it.

Without speaking Miley pushed her arms up and quickly pulled the tab on her bottle of water before squirting it into Diesel's face.

Diesel groaned. "What was that for?"

"You can't breathe fire when you're wet," Miley replied with a slight shrug. "It's common knowledge."

Diesel laughed. Flat out laughed at her. "Where did you get your 'common knowledge' information from?" he managed out of his laughter as he quickly pushed himself up and shifted at the same time.

Miley squeaked pushing herself backward toward a rock behind her for support. She was still getting use to the giant dragon beast. She stared at his beauty wide eyed.

He turned his head slightly toward the lake beside them and let out a massive ball of fire from his mouth. "All lies mate," he purred. His voice was thickly laced with the strange accent that Miley had kept forgetting to mention.

"Why do you have that strange accent?" she asked curiously as she stood up and rubbed her hand across the dragon's nose.

He breathed in her scent closing his eyes and purring. "Different language," he told her nonchalantly.

"You speak a different language?" Miley replied confused.

"Yes dear," he murmured nuzzling her neck. "Your hormones smell different."

Diesel had finally just given up on his work for the day. He took his time to enjoy the last moments before June's boat was due to arrive by kissing Miley and calming her and himself down.

By the time they had soothed their playfulness enough go back to the house, June's boat was due to arrive in fifteen minutes. "Diesel," Miley moaned.

"I have to get some clothes woman, before we give June a heart attack." Diesel let out a breath and shook his head.

He had yet to understand what that strange new delicious scent was coming from is mate. Diesel pulled on a pair of shorts and chuckled as he walked to Miley stomping her foot.

"Come on, silly woman."

Chapter 62

"Miley you are just absolutely glowing!" June smiled as she wrapped her arms around Miley's waist. "When is the wedding?"

Diesel smiled, "another month. We're giving enough time for as many people to get here as we invited, such as Miley's friend Morgan," Diesel told her.

"Oh thank goodness," June beamed. "I would hate to see you get too much further into that pregnancy when you get married."

Miley gasped. "Excuse me," she sputtered.

"I knew I could smell something different," Diesel grinned.

"I'm not pregnant," Miley scoffed, "I'm still on the pill."

Diesel leaned over and pressed his lips to Miley's ear, "Dragon as a mate love."

Her eyes went wide. It had finally hit Miley; she had been so busy moving and getting settled that she had completely forgotten about missing her period. "Come along darling, I don't think you should be on your feet all day," June said stepping up urging Miley forward.

June had proven to be a wonderful addition to the home. Diesel had actually intended on her just being there as a friend and motherly figure to Miley, yet even in June's old age she refused to sit down and rest all day.

The weeks flew by and before any of them knew it, the wedding was upon them. Morgan and Orion had finally came to the island bringing along with them Roger, Miley's father for the wedding.

Quite a surprise to Miley, she had been pregnant. Very pregnant actually. She had been three months pregnant of the six-month dragon pregnancy or nine-month human pregnancy.

Her belly had grown quite round within the last month and she was worried she wasn't going to fit into the beautiful white sundress June and her had picked out.

The wedding was simple, but elegant. White lilies and yellow roses, decorated the tables. Each of the clan had helped set up the wedding in some way or form. The little children, which there was not much off had helped woman hang bows while the strong men had helped set up the tables.

The ceremony was held on the beach and the reception was beneath a pavilion that Diesel had specially built for the occasion. When Miley had remembered back to that day, she was so happy that everything had turned out so beautifully.

Her father had come to visit and witness the wedding along with giving away his daughter, yet Samantha refused to budge and wouldn't show up.

Chapter 63

"Are you alright daddy?" Miley asked. It was now the middle of the summer's blaring heat and Miley was five and a half months pregnant.

"Yes my daughter. I am just thinking if I made the right decision leaving your mother." Roger contemplated.

"I'm sorry you had to choose," Miley sighed her hand rubbed unconsciously against her stomach as she carefully dropped her aching body onto a hammock.

"Oh don't be like that, Miley. It was bound to happen someday anyway. I just am wondering about life right now," Roger smiled sadly. He was trying to decide if he should stay on the island with his daughter or stay living in the town that was now filled with rumors.

"Well you know you can always stay here with us," Diesel said coming out of the house.

Roger turned his head toward Diesel and chuckled. "Thank you for the offer, but I'm not really sure what I want to do right now. I think I'll stay here until my grandbaby is born and then I'll go from there."

"Well that's fine also," Diesel nodded. "It's time we get going love, the doctor's waiting on us."

Miley groaned. She was growing more and more tired as the days passed and she really did not want to get up. "Come on darling," Diesel chuckled as he reached forward and wrapped an arm around his mate's growing waist.

"This baby is getting so big. I don't think I can make it to nine months," Miley moaned as the couple began to walk back up the path to the front of the house.

"That is what we are going to check on today," Diesel reminded her.

"Oh! I forgot!" Miley brightened up as she struggled to move herself faster.

"Wow, feisty, slow on down!" Diesel chuckled as he caught up to his mate with ease. "If you insist on going so fast I'll just carry you."

Before Miley could answer, Diesel tucked an arm under Miley's bare thighs and lifted her up into his strong arms. Even with a massive pregnancy belly, he carried her as if she weighed nothing.

"I don't think I can ever get use to your strength," Miley giggled as she rubbed her face against Diesel's strong chest.

"It's about time you got here," the doctor groaned out. "I do have others whom have to wait until after your appointment."

"I'm sorry," Miley mumbled shamefully.

"Doc," Diesel growled. "Miley, you are the alpha female. Everyone will be second to you," he nodded her head softly as Diesel settled her feet back onto the floor.

"Yes, uh... pardon me alpha. I have just had a busy day. I'm sorry I was disrespectful." The doctor apologized helping Miley up onto the examination table.

"Let's see what we have going on," the doctor muttered to himself. As he ran the monitor across Miley's belly, he gasped.

It had been years since such an amazing thing had happened. "What!" Diesel growled. "What is it?"

"Calm down Diesel," Miley said softly though her words were shaky and worried.

"It's nothing bad. I promise. It's just that…," the doctor muttered. "It's just…"

"Spit it out doc before I knock it out of you!" Diesel snarled.

"Yes uh sorry alpha," the doctor said ducking his head. "It's just that your baby is a very rare event."

Chapter 64

Diesel had been concentrating so hard on his work lately, but nothing ever seemed to get done. Orion had assumed his beta duties and was filling in more and more by the day for his alpha.

Thinking back, Diesel could not believe his ears when the doctor had told him the baby was going to be going through dragon pregnancy terms. There was only a matter of days and their baby was going to be born.

He could only wish that the beautiful creature growing within his mate would become like him, yet that would not happen. It had been two weeks and the baby still had not decided on coming out.

Diesel found it hard to do any work, without Miley being right at his side. She had been tired this morning and he really did not want to drag her out of bed just to lie on the couch in his office all day.

Miley's scream broke him out of his thoughts and he bolted upright. Sprinting down the hall and up the stairs with his inhuman speed Diesel burst through the door. "Miley what's the matter baby? Are you alright?"

"The baby it's on the way!" Miley cried. "My water broke and contractions started," she panted, as another contraction began to rake through her body.

The pain was nearly intolerable. "What do I do?" Diesel replied. He frantically rushed to his mate's side, holding her up as he walked her to a spot to sit. "How far apart are they? The doctor said to let him know when the contractions were close."

"They're close," Miley groaned out.

Miley's scream had attracted many others to the room and now June, Morgan, and Orion were all standing at the door worriedly looking in. "What can I do?" Orion asked.

"Get the doctor. I'll carry her to the maternity room," Diesel barked out. He had scooped his arms around Miley and lifted her up.

"We're not going to make it," Miley moaned as the pain begun again.

"I'll make it darling. Hold on," Diesel sighed. He had wished she would have told him earlier but he knew why she hadn't. "How long have you been in pain?" he worried.

"We're almost there!" Diesel grunted out as Miley squeezed his arm trying to ease another contraction.

"Oh my goodness," the doctor breathed. "How long has she been in labor?"

"I don't know…" Diesel mumbled.

"Four hours," Miley whimpered.

"Well let's see how you're doing," the doctor shook his head. At Diesel's disgruntled face and began to examine Miley.

Chapter 65

Diesel sighed looking down at the small little baby in his arms. "What is it?" Miley asked anxiously.

"She won't be like me," he half frowned. "But you are always a beautiful alternative…"

"What do you mean?" Miley questioned her brows furrowed together as she looked down at the little creature that looked just as stunningly beautiful as her daddy.

"Don't worry about it love," Diesel whispered softly.

"Diesel, tell me…"

"Females aren't generally born with the gene," Diesel told her sadly.

"She won't be a dragon," Miley murmured.

"No. There has not been a female dragon born in three hundred years. Our species bloodline is getting more and more diluted with human blood every generation and therefore losing a part of our dragon a little at a time," Diesel told her.

"Oh Diesel," Miley cooed as she tried to sit up from the bed.

"Rest," he said pressing her down softly. "Only time will tell."

"Why are you so upset? Aren't you happy for us?" Miley whimpered.

Diesel just walked away silently. "It's not that he's not happy love…" Orion said softly. "It's that he won't have an heir…"

He was interrupted by the most ear piercing call he had ever heard.

It was shrill, loud, and longing like sound. "What the hell was that?" Miley choked as she stared down at the bubbly little baby who made the noise.

Diesel had stopped dead in his tracks, turned around, and was now wearing a massive smile, "An alpha dragon calling to her clan that she is born."

The End

Hope you enjoyed the Island of Dragons by Lindsey Owens

Please check out
http://dreambigpublishing.net
for more info on the books in our collection.